NEVER A BRIDE

Leanne Banks

A KISMET™ Romance

METEOR PUBLISHING CORPORATION
Bensalem, Pennsylvania

A heartfelt thanks to:

Kate Duffy for pulling me out of the slush pile.

Tom and Betty Minyard for sending me flowers *before* I bloomed.

Carolyn Greene and Mary Anderson for contributing lots of blue ink and encouragement.

Tony and J.C. for believing when I didn't.

LEANNE BANKS

As a little girl, Leanne Banks became a fan of romance when she first heard the story of Cinderella. After marrying her own Prince Charming and having a son and daughter, she turned her creative energies toward writing. *Never A Bride* is her first novel and now that the writing bug has bitten, Leanne promises "the best is yet to come!"

ONE

"Congratulations! You are the fiftieth woman to join us for Strike a Match Night at Grocery Town, and you've just won a date to see the Broadway hit musical *Cats*, and dinner at Francois' restaurant. How do you feel?"

Cassie Warner stared blankly at the jubilant man with the microphone. A date to see *Cats*? Then, as she saw the banners advertising the Singles' Strike a Match Night posted around the grocery store, she groaned in comprehension. As a gimmick, the store had arranged a night for singles to meet each other, complete with prizes of dates or free groceries. Why couldn't she win the groceries?

"She's speechless!" The radio DJ motioned her over to a table. "You go right over there, doll, and give them the pertinent information. Your date is over there, too."

Cassie started to protest as she pointed at her legs. "But, I just wanted to buy some panty hose. I don't—"

The announcer interrupted, giving her a gentle shove. "I know you're excited. But we'll take care of you. Just go on over to the table, honey."

Chafing under his pushy attitude, she glanced over her shoulder at the DJ with narrowed eyes. Doll. Honey. But he'd already begun babbling at some other unfortunate soul.

Sighing, she walked over to the table where a woman waited expectantly. She really needed to get this cleared up or she would be late for her friend Anne's wedding rehearsal. And though she'd love to see *Cats*, she wasn't the least bit interested in a blind date.

The woman at the table wore an expression of envy. "Boy, are you lucky," she said. "You got the best-looking hunk here tonight. He doesn't want to go on the date, but maybe you'll be able to talk him into it. Let's get your name, address, and telephone number so you two can set up your meeting time."

Taking in the woman's appearance, Cassie pondered what kind of man appealed to someone with spiked fuschia hair and earrings resembling daggers. An axe murderer or Hell's Angel? She began to protest again, but stopped when she heard a deep masculine voice tinged with frustration.

"There must be a hundred guys here tonight who'd love to have a prepaid blind date. I'm not one of them. You're the store manager. Can't you bend the rules a little and give this prize to someone else?"

Though she agreed with his argument, she felt affronted by the way he'd said the word prize, as if his date would be just the opposite.

Cassie turned to look at him and caught his gaze with her own. He strode toward her and held out his hand. "I'm Joshua Daniels. Are you my date for *Cats*?"

She automatically shook his hand. "Yes, but I have almost as much interest in blind dates as you. I've just been trying to persuade these people to bestow this prize on someone else."

His keen dark eyes wore an expression of measured concentration, as if after seeing her he was reconsidering his options. Dressed in a navy suit, he looked like the all-American success story: about six feet tall, thick brown hair, nice square jaw, and a cleft in his chin.

The only thing she didn't like about him was the way his dark brown eyes were traveling down her legs with masculine appreciation. He looked like the intense kind who couldn't resist a challenge, and Cassie instinctively avoided intense men. She carefully selected a more biddable type of man for her platonic dates, and this man looked anything but biddable.

She turned from him to the woman at the table. "There's been some mistake. I only came here to buy a pair of—"

The woman shook her head firmly. "Oh, there's been no mistake. You're the fiftieth single woman to walk through that door tonight. There were two people counting. Now, what's your name?"

Sputtering in protest, Cassie opened her mouth, only to have him pull at her hand.

Joshua held her hand firmly in his own and she had to resist the urge to jerk it away. Her skin seemed acutely sensitive to his touch.

In a low voice, Joshua nonchalantly negotiated with her. "There's no convincing them you're not interested.

I've already tried. We could end up being here all night." He pointed to her dress. "And, you look like you have other places to go."

Wary at his change in attitude, she said, "But I thought you didn't like blind dates."

He smiled and shrugged. "It's not a blind date, anymore. We've met."

When he smiled, Cassie got her second indication that this man was genetically designed to destroy a woman's natural defenses. She purposely removed her hand from his.

Still, he appeared reasonable enough, and it was only one evening. . . . Cassie studied his face once more. A practical man. Definitely not an axe murderer. Turning to the woman, she said, "When is this date?"

"Next Saturday. I need your name, phone number, and address."

Cassie sighed. She truly hated blind dates, but she didn't have time for a debate right now. Perhaps she could find a way out of it later. Rapidly, she said, "Cassie Warner, 555–1010, 203 Maple Lane. Can I go now?"

Writing furiously, the woman nodded. Cassie turned and heard Joshua Daniel's amused voice call to her. "See you next week, Cassie."

Snatching the package of panty hose, Cassie slammed her car door and raced to the back of the church. She would have liked to linger over the spring foliage, but she didn't have time. She barely noticed the blooming azaleas and lilies so common to North Carolina.

She peeked through the backdoor. Pleased to find the hall empty, she hurried to the ladies' room. She grimaced at the sight of her ripped hose. If only she could have used the extra pair she kept at her store. But black hose didn't coordinate well with peach, aqua, and white lace. She pushed the ruined nylons down and slipped off her shoes. Hopping on one foot, she stretched on the new pair.

Taking a deep breath, she looked in the mirror. She brushed her shoulder length blonde hair, smoothed lipstick onto her generous mouth, and rolled on a dab of perfume. Eyeing her reflection critically, she raised an eyebrow. It would have to do. Cassie knew she was flushed and rattled. But she wasn't the bride, so no one would be looking at her anyway. If she hadn't been so unnerved at the prospect of being in this wedding, she would have been on her toes enough to find a way out of that silly blind date she'd committed herself to.

She left the bathroom and quietly opened the sanctuary door. A group of men laughing among themselves sat in the front pews. She walked in the direction of the bridesmaids sitting on the other side of the church.

In the front pew, Joshua Daniels smiled wryly at his two longtime friends' laughter. He'd been set up. His first night back in town, and these two clowns had conned him into picking up a few necessities from the grocery store. The guys had wanted to play a practical joke on Tom, the groom. Oblivious to the singles madhouse inside the grocery store, Joshua had volunteered to get the supplies and found himself snatched by the ecstatic DJ upon entering the door.

The only saving grace was the woman. When she'd fixed him with a suspicious glare from those aquamarine eyes, he'd practically bitten the inside of his cheek off to keep from laughing at the whole situation.

"Was she as big as a barn, Joshua? What's her name?" Fred teased.

"No, she wasn't as big as a barn. To tell you the truth, I should probably thank you for sending me in there." Joshua smiled benignly.

"You're kidding," Fred said in astonishment. "You got a peach? What'd she look like? What's her name?"

"Honey blonde hair, blue-green eyes," Joshua paused. "Nice, long legs. Oh, and her name is Cassie something."

"Cassie," Jack choked. "Cassie Warner?"

Joshua's eyebrows drew together in a frown as he surveyed the surprise written on his friends' faces. He wondered what he'd gotten himself into this time. "Yeah, I think that's her name. Why? What's wrong with her?"

Jack blew out a stream of breath. "Nothing's wrong with her. As a matter-of-fact, just about every male over the age of eighteen in our fair city of St. James would give his right arm for a date with Cassie Warner."

Joshua relaxed and smiled. "So, what's the problem?"

Jack and Fred exchanged a knowing look and Fred replied, "Cassie's a beautiful girl . . . with a very annoying habit."

Stumped, Joshua tried to imagine what could possibly be annoying about Cassie Warner. "Okay, I give. What annoying habit?"

"Whenever Cassie senses that a man is getting too, uh, interested in her, she fixes him up with a friend." Fred grinned sheepishly. "I speak from experience. I went out with her a few times. When I started calling her everyday, she fixed me up with Kim. Not that I have any complaints about Kim. We've been seeing each other for six months. Cassie did me a real favor.''

Jack nodded. "Same here. Only she fixed me up with Marie.''

Tom smirked at Fred and Jack. "You should have seen the way these two clowns practically stumbled over themselves when they were dating her. It was pathetic. And Cassie hardly noticed them.''

Joshua frowned. "She sounds a little snobbish.''

"Actually, that's not part of the problem,'' said Jack. "She's as nice as she is beautiful. It's kinda hard to hate someone for rejecting you when she makes it seem like it was your idea.'' He looked over at the latest arrival and cocked his head. "Speaking of Cassie, she just walked in.''

Surprised and confused, Joshua asked, "What's she doing here?''

Jack shrugged. "She's a bridesmaid. She's good friends with Anne, the bride.''

Joshua watched the lovely woman smile and talk with her friends and felt a challenge rise within him. She exuded a natural sensuality that she probably didn't even realize she possessed. Her femininity beckoned to him and he saw no reason to avoid the sensual magic he felt sure they'd share. "Thanks for the tip, boys. I hope Cassie's run out of available friends. Because if she hasn't, we're in for a rough ride.''

The wedding director clapped her hands together and told everyone to sit down while she explained the order for the service. Cassie had relaxed with her friends' warm conversation. Glancing around the room, she mentally named all the occupants until her gaze fell on him. Him! Apprehension made her nerves taut. She nudged Kim and whispered, "Who's the new guy beside Fred?"

Kim glanced affectionately at Fred, then whispered, "Joshua Daniels. Isn't he a dream? He grew up in St. James. He's been living in Raleigh, but I hear he's moving back to open up his own business. He's got this bad boy reputation, but Fred says he's come back so everyone can see what a success he is." Kim smiled impishly. "Can I fix you up?"

Shaking her head, Cassie answered dryly, "I don't think that'll be necessary."

The director waved the women to the back of the church and positioned the men in the front. Smiling at Anne's shining eyes, Cassie squeezed her friend's hand. "I'm so happy for you and Tom."

"I am, too. We've only been engaged for three months, but I feel like I've been waiting for this forever." The petite bride-to-be hugged Cassie.

When the organ played the procession and the bridesmaids walked down the aisle, Cassie steadfastly ignored Joshua Daniels' eyes. She felt embarrassed about their first encounter and off balance at being involved in this wedding, so she wasn't her natural, friendly self. She needed time to figure out how to handle Joshua. But time wasn't on her side. And before she knew it, she was being escorted back down the aisle by him.

"Fancy meeting you here," he murmured in that deep voice. "I've known these people for ages. Where have they been hiding you?"

Momentarily distracted by his nearness, she smiled. "I could ask you the same question."

Two points. She'd given him a smile, though he

could tell she felt awkward by the way she drummed her free hand against her thigh.

Among other things, Joshua was . . . curious. It was completely puzzling to him why such an attractive single woman would have no interest in romance. Never having been able to resist puzzles, Joshua knew he would have to figure Cassie out. Inhaling her enticing floral fragrance and feeling her soft hand on his arm, he predicted the experience could be quite enjoyable. He glanced down at her legs. "I see you finally got your nylons."

Nylons. Date. This was a perfect opportunity to get out of the date. "Yes, and that's the most I've ever gone through to get a pair of stockings. I thought I'd never get out of there. Joshua, about that date, I don't think—"

Cutting her off, he said, "Don't worry about it. We can work out the arrangements later." Then, he lowered his voice in a conspiratorial manner, "Can you keep a secret?" He watched her nod with a curious expression on her face. "I was picking up materials for a practical joke we're playing on Tom tonight. All three of us owe him for something he did to us during a softball game eight years ago."

She frowned. "Yes, but the date . . ." Then, sidetracked, astonishment played across her features. "You're paying him back for a joke he played on you eight years ago."

"With vengeance," he said emphatically. "The experience of itching powder in my underwear is etched in my memory for life."

She laughed at that, a delicious tinkling sound that rippled along his skin. The sensation of her nearness was wonderful and he resolved to experience it again. He tried to think of how to prolong the moment, but the wedding director shooed the ushers up to the front once more, and Cassie slid her arm from his.

The rest of rehearsal passed smoothly, and the group bade friendly farewells to each other as they departed. It wasn't until she dressed for bed that Cassie realized she hadn't managed to break the date. When she slept that night, a man's face invaded her dreams. A handsome face with laughing brown eyes, strong bones, and cleft chin.

The next evening, Cassie slipped into the aqua off-the-shoulder gown Anne had selected for the bridesmaids. Animated chatter and nervous giggles filled the room the women used for dressing. Cassie's nervousness came from memories of a similar time in her life.

Being jilted the day before her wedding at age nineteen by her high-school sweetheart had left her with a feeling of terror about wedding ceremonies. The humiliation had been overwhelming. Although her mother had phoned the guests with the news, Cassie had returned every single gift, and bore pitying glances with each visit. News that her fiance had eloped with someone else traveled fast.

That's when she decided to move to St. James. And St. James had been good to her. She'd finished college here, opened her store, and formed a circle of close friends. No great shakes in the romance department, but that was fine with Cassie.

Even after six years, the idea of a wedding still brought a clammy feeling to her skin. Cassie would rather be sitting in a dentist's chair, getting a root canal, than be a part of this wedding. But Anne had been a wonderful friend and college roommate, and she would have been crushed if Cassie had refused to participate in the wedding.

"Cassie, are you okay?" Kim studied her. "You look pale."

Cassie forced a smile and placed a hand to her cheek. "I guess I need more blusher. How's our bride holding up?"

Kim looked at the bubbling bride in front of the mirror. "I'd say the question is how do we keep her on the ground. She's like a rocket ready to blast off."

At that moment, the wedding director peeked through the door and gave a five-minute warning. The anticipation in the room was palpable as Cassie blotted her lipstick. When a messenger delivered a last-minute gift of pearls from the groom, Cassie watched her friend dab at tears of joy. Banishing a trace of envy she felt at the sweet gesture, Cassie fastened the necklace at Anne's neck and gave her a hug.

The old church looked dressed for the wedding with flowers on the pews and the altar. The only illumination was candlelight.

Taking her turn down the aisle, Cassie studied the faces at the front of the church. The groom looked tense, yet resolute. Fred and Jack attempted a serious countenance, but their grins escaped.

Then, there was Joshua. Dashing in a black tux, his natural tan contrasted nicely with the stiff white shirt. He looked solid and steady. Their eyes met and held. Cassie tensed at the absorbing way he watched her. His gaze remained steady. He had intense, expressive eyes. For one wild moment, she wondered what they looked like when they were warm with desire, glazed with passion.

Now, where did that thought come from? She was satisfied with her life. She attributed her wayward thoughts to the occasion and dismissed them. Weddings always seemed to stir up a myriad of emotions within her. Drawing a fortifying breath, she took her place at the front.

The sweet ceremony passed in a blur. When Joshua escorted her to the back of the church, she was acutely aware of his closeness. Her pulse increased, and she found the sensation both pleasant and disturbing. His arm was strong beneath her hand, but she felt confused by the intensity of her reaction to him and quickly moved away.

After much clowning from the bridal party, the photographer took pictures, and everyone left for the reception at a nearby inn.

As Cassie danced with Anne's father, she looked longingly at the delicious spread of food on the tables. She'd been too busy at her shop to eat anything since lunch and if her stomach growled much louder, she'd be competing with the band. Just when the number ended, she turned to the food, only to have Tom's father ask her to dance. Not wanting to be rude, she chatted with him while he spun her around the room.

Joshua watched Cassie's hungry gaze repeatedly return to the tables of food. He grinned at her dilemma of hunger competing against politeness, and an idea came to mind. He filled a plate with everything he could possibly fit on it, lifted a glass of champagne punch from a passing waiter's tray, and waited for the end of the song. Hiding the plate behind his back, he approached her.

Cassie looked at Joshua with resignation. "I suppose you want to dance."

Nodding, Joshua presented her with the food. "After you eat."

She smiled and took the plate as they walked to the chairs. "You must have heard my stomach growling."

Chuckling, he shook his head. "No, your eyes gave you away. I was sure you were going to eat some poor man's boutonniere if you didn't get food soon."

She laughed, eyeing the food ravenously, then noticed he didn't have a plate. "Don't you want something?"

"I've already had mine. You go ahead."

Needing no further encouragement, Cassie tasted and savored the various hors d'oeuvres Joshua had piled on her plate, occasionally commenting on a particular delicacy.

He would have been content merely to watch her. The silky aqua dress she wore fitted her curves lovingly, emphasizing her tiny waist. Still, it was her bare, satiny shoulders that drew his attention. She reminded him of a beautiful package all wrapped up in ruffled pastel.

And he wanted to unwrap her. Joshua shook his head at his thoughts. If she knew what he was thinking, she'd probably throw that plate in his face and run. When he asked her about her job, she gestured to her full mouth and he laughed.

"How about if I take a rain check on your life history, and give you mine while you're eating?" Joshua asked.

He acknowledged her enthusiastic nod. "I was raised

in St. James. But I went away to college in Chapel Hill. While I was working on my M.B.A., a fraternity brother and I decided to start up a business servicing the university and small businesses—sort of a hodge-podge of copying services. It was so successful that we've opened two other stores. St. James has the perfect market for our business, so we'll open our fourth here." Cassie appeared interested so he continued. "The key to our business, like many, is location—downtown, yet still close to the college."

Cassie swallowed her last bite. "Good luck. It sounds like a great idea, but I'm sure you know down-town property is at a premium, unless you want to buy." She watched his satisfied smile. "You want to buy?"

"I closed this week. And the current renter will be moving out soon." He looked down at her empty plate in amazement. "Where'd you put all that food?"

Cassie laughed, "It's nine o'clock and I haven't had anything to eat since lunch. I've had a very high metab-olism since I was a teenager." Her eyes twinkled when she solemnly informed him, "My father had to get a second job to pay the grocery bill when I turned four-teen. At least, that's what he would tell you. Of course, he'd leave out the fact that he had two six-foot teenage sons who played football."

He whistled softly. "Were you the baby and the only daughter?" He watched her nod. "I'll bet they dressed you in pink ruffles and scared your dates to death."

"That's right." Cassie gave her plate to a waiter. "I took ballet until I grew four inches in one year. Then I ran track."

"Track?" Joshua puzzled.

"When you've got two giants for big brothers, you've got two choices: You're either very strong or very fast." She looked at him curiously. "So, what about you? Do you have any brothers or sisters?"

Shaking his head, he wore a pained expression. "No. I'm the only child . . . of a minister. By moving to Chapel Hill, I spared my parents the embarrassment of witnessing my college years. But I don't think they've ever recovered from the amount of time I spent in the principal's office in high school."

"I bet they're proud of you now, and thrilled that you're moving back to St. James," she said.

His smile faded. "My mother is. My father died three years ago."

"Oh." Cassie's eyes reflected her sympathy. "I'm sorry. I'm sure it's difficult. I've never lost anyone who was very close to me."

He studied her intently, comprehending why most men would want a relationship with her. She was shy without being coy, and she was funny, tender, and knock-your-socks-off sexy. Listening to the slow tune the band was playing, he held out his hand to Cassie and grinned lazily. "I didn't take ballet, but I think I can handle a few turns around the dance floor. Are you ready?"

Cassie hesitated. He'd been a perfect gentleman, no sly innuendos, no groping. Still, there was something about the way he'd looked at her a few moments before; the same way she'd looked at the plate of food he'd given her. Hungry. The expression in his eyes had been so fleeting she may well have imagined it. Chastising herself for her imagination, Cassie gave him her hand. For pete's sake, the man was just trying to be friendly.

Her earlier impression of him must have been a delusion based on her distress over being in this wedding. Furthermore, she could use the dance as an opportunity to tactfully bow out of the scheduled date.

He held her closely with one hand firmly on the small of her back and his other hand clasping hers near his chest.

Now she understood why she'd been hesitant. Their swaying movements occasionally allowed her body to brush against his, heightening her awareness of his masculine form. She sensed a restrained strength about him.

His large hands held her firmly, yet gently. This preacher's kid may never have taken ballet, but somewhere along the way, he'd learned how to dance in a way that made a woman feel wholly feminine.

Inhaling deeply, Cassie realized that he took over her senses. Even his scent was compelling; the combination of his masculine essence with musky aftershave. Keeping her head averted, she felt her blood race through her veins and her breasts tighten. An ache settled low in her belly. She couldn't let him see her face; her arousal would be too apparent. He'd neither done nor said anything suggestive, yet she felt seduced. Lord, how long had it been since she felt this way?

Sweet agony, thought Joshua. Holding her womanly body a breath away from his was sweet agony. Her soft hair tickled his chin, and her small hand was warm within his own. Sucking in his breath, he felt her breasts brush briefly against his chest, then move away. He couldn't hold his breath for the entire song, so he released it slowly. He longed to touch her bare skin, but he couldn't think of an excuse.

Studying her averted head, he wondered if she felt

the same way. Or was he the only one enduring the torture of their nearness? Joshua was way past curious about Cassie Warner. The song ended. And when she lifted her smoky eyes to his, he knew with certainty that Cassie would be his greatest exercise in restraint. He kept one of her hands folded in his own. "May I give you a ride home tonight?"

Cassie swallowed, breathless with the intensity of his gaze. "No. I brought my own car. But, thanks." She tried to think of something else to say, but his closeness seemed to have impaired her mental abilities.

He studied her again. "That's okay. I'll call you about our date next week."

Slipping her hand from his, she nodded yes when she should have been shaking her head no. She felt both relieved and bereft as his warmth was separated from her. Though she couldn't physically feel his touch, she still felt it emotionally. This man's effect on her was dangerous.

Panicky over her loss of control, she decided she must leave. There was more to Joshua Daniels than what met the eye. Although what met the eye wasn't that bad either. She spoke huskily, "I've got to go help Anne. She'll be leaving soon."

"I'll call," he said. He watched her leave quickly, almost as if the hounds of hell raced after her.

After toasts to the bride and groom, the newlyweds prepared to go. Tom tossed the garter to a group of joking men. When Anne gathered all the unattached women around to catch her bouquet, Joshua noticed Cassie's reluctance. They practically had to drag her into the group. She folded her hands behind her back. And when Anne's bouquet landed at Cassie's feet, she shuffled backwards to let some other eager woman grab it. Stroking his chin thoughtfully, Joshua's curiosity was aroused anew. This woman allowed no pretense of commitment to a man in her life. Now, if he could just figure out why.

TWO

Shaking off the morning rain, Cassie flicked on the lights to her store. The store was always a source of delight for her. Well, almost always. She honestly didn't enjoy the bookkeeping aspect of owning her own business. And doing inventory presented a real problem. She found herself spending far too much time exclaiming over each item, almost as if they were Christmas presents beneath her tree. The items in her shop ranged from hummingbird feeders to antique lace.

She'd worked hard to build her clientele. The name, Discriminating Pleasures, had brought in many curious shoppers who found the store lived up to its name. The idea was spawned by her difficulty locating unique gifts for her family and friends for holidays and birthdays.

Upon her graduation from college, her father had offered her a gift of a new sports car or money. She'd combined the money with a small inheritance she received from a distant uncle and lived on a shoestring budget for three years. Finally, she was experiencing success. And none too soon; her twelve-year-old Honda Civic seemed to demand more from her pocketbook with each passing month.

She leased the shop with an option to buy from an elderly man, although there was no way she could have afforded it. She paid a steep rent, but the location was just what she needed; right in the middle of the downtown business district. The store offered convenience to all those businessmen and secretaries who needed to pick up that special something on their lunch hours.

St. James was unusual in that most of the owners of the downtown buildings didn't rent out their space. The owners used the buildings to operate their own businesses. Therefore, rentals were at a premium. The thought struck her that her area would be perfect for Joshua Daniels' new business. Perhaps he would be a new neighbor. Joshua Daniels had crossed her mind more than once since the wedding. He'd been friendly and easy to talk to. She was tempted to go out with him as they'd planned. Still, she felt uncomfortable with the emotions that had stirred within her when they danced.

He seemed like a man with both feet on the ground. Perhaps Joshua was someone with whom she could enjoy an easy friendship, without the romance that tended to complicate things. Cassie shook her head at her thoughts; she was being presumptuous in thinking that Joshua harbored romantic notions toward her. The only overtures he had made had been bringing her a plate of food and dancing with her once. Brushing her daydreams aside, she turned to the mail.

Bills, catalogs, a sweepstakes, and a letter from a local law firm. Cassie ripped it open. A few months ago, her landlord had announced his plans to sell the building. When Cassie told him she couldn't afford to buy, he promised to try to find a buyer who would be willing to continue renting to her. Although she felt uneasy with the arrangement, she'd decided to trust her landlord. After all, he'd done nothing to arouse her suspicions before. Wondering if he'd finally sold it, Cassie eagerly read the letter.

Her stomach sank. The new owner wished to take possession of the building as soon as possible. Although they were required to allow her to finish out her lease, Danburg, Inc., offered a monetary incentive, along with their assistance in finding her a new location, if she moved within sixty days.

She covered her mouth in horror. Sixty days!

The bell on her door tinkled, signalling the arrival of her part-time sales clerk, Maggie Ames. "Good morning, Cassie. That rain's just pouring down out there. Makes my rheumatism remind me that I've turned sixty this year. Landsakes, girl! You're so pale, you look as if you've seen a ghost."

"I think I have Maggie. My own!" Cassie waved the letter and wailed, "My new landlord wants me out of this building within sixty days. He's not renewing my lease."

"Oh my, are you sure you read that right?"

In a daze, she finished reading the letter. It seemed that the new owner of her building was a company by the name of Danburg, Inc. The letter went on to say that the partners of Danburg, Inc., would be in touch with her within the next few days. Along with her past landlord, they would be happy to provide her with a good reference. How gracious, thought Cassie.

What in the world was she going to do? Perhaps she could persuade them to allow her to stay a little longer, she thought hopefully. But the tone of the letter was firm; they expected her out by the end of her lease, if not, before.

"Two months," Cassie repeated. How could she possibly find a comparable place for her store in two months? It had taken six months to find this one. "I'll just have to call this lawyer and see if I can get an extension."

"Cassie, maybe it's not that bad. The new landlord might be willing to let you rent for a little while." Maggie's concerned gaze followed Cassie's pacing from one end of the store to the other.

Cassie frowned and shook her head. "No. Whoever is buying this building has plans for it. Maggie, please watch the store. I've got a few phone calls to make." With that, she whirled into her office.

When she came back out an hour later, she was even more glum. Maggie clucked over Cassie. "Did you get in touch with the lawyer?"

"Yes. He said he understands my problem, but his client is determined to move in as quickly as possible." Cassie winced. "I also called my lawyer and realtor. My lawyer promised to look over my contract, but he said I'd better plan on moving. And to top it off, my realtor informed me that very few rental properties are available downtown. She said it could be six months to a year before there's a suitable opening."

Sighing, Cassie looked around the beloved shop she'd poured so much of herself into. The idea of starting over seemed overwhelming. Chin up, she scolded herself, you've been through other tough times, you'll make it through this.

"Maggie, we'll think of something. Perhaps, the new owner will let me rent it long enough to find another place. I've worked too hard to let this get me down."

Maggie smiled at her young employer as she chewed her customary piece of gum. "That's the spirit, Cassie. You're a clever girl. I know you'll think of something."

Her confidence lifted at the older woman's affirmation. And she thanked her lucky stars for hiring Maggie two years earlier. The widow had become enchanted with Cassie's store. With Maggie visiting the store frequently, it made perfect sense to hire the lonely woman. The older woman became a hit with the customers with her sunny disposition and eagerness to help. And the relationship between Maggie and Cassie had grown into a warm friendship.

Cassie placed her hand on Maggie's shoulder. "Thanks for the vote of confidence. Now, if I can just live up to it." She looked around the store. "I think I'll finish up the inventory of the homemade dolls. They'll keep my mind off that letter." Grabbing her inventory form, she moved to the dolls.

She spent the next few hours greeting customers and cataloging the dolls. Since lunch was often her busiest time, she usually took her own very early or very late. At three o'clock, she was preparing to grab a bite when Joshua Daniels and another man walked through the door.

Joshua saw the smile of welcome on Cassie's face and almost winced. At the reception, they'd never gotten around to discussing Cassie's business, and since his realtor had handled most of the details, he'd only known the name of the shop he was going to remove from his building. He'd had no idea her store and the building he bought were one and the same. Her curious gaze encompassed his partner, Ken Blomburg, and he wondered how he was going to handle this sticky situation until Ken spoke.

"Hello, I'm Ken Blomburg with Danburg, Inc." The young man pushed his glasses back on his nose with one hand and extended the other to Cassie. "We want to discuss your moving date, so we can make plans for the contractors. Shall we go to your office?"

Cassie felt sick, and shocked, and angry all at once. Her moving date! She'd just received the letter this morning. Briefly touching Mr. Blomburg's hand, she fixed a frosty smile on Joshua. "What a pleasure to see you again, Mr. Daniels. I was informed just this morning that my building had been sold, so I haven't decided on a moving date." Cassie said sweetly, "As you can see, we do have customers here right now." She led them to the door and opened it. "Perhaps you can come back when we're closed." *Hopefully, I won't be here*, she thought. "Now, if you'll excuse me, I need to attend to some work in my office." She seriously considered giving each of them a swift kick, but restrained herself.

Seething inwardly, she sped to her office with Maggie staring after her. She closed the door and covered her face with her hands in disbelief. One of her major stumbling blocks in life had been her reluctance to rock the boat or do anything that would hurt someone's feelings.

When her ex-fiance had asked her to cancel the

arrangements for their wedding, she had done it. When someone asked her out for a date and she didn't want to go, she went to extremes to keep from hurting him. Hating the idea of hurting anyone's feelings, Cassie had even fixed up a few very nice men with some of her friends. And with fine results. She'd long ago accepted the fact that she preferred to avoid confrontation. Cassie justified her attitude by reasoning that it took a higher level of intellect and creativity to handle life's rough spots with poise and calm.

Yet, she'd practically kicked two men, the owners of her building, no less, out of her store without batting an eyelash.

Feeling foolish over her daydreams of Joshua Daniels, she picked up her inventory records and threw them at the wall. Was he romancing her while he was stealing her store right out from underneath her? She wondered if he could have possibly known that the property he bought housed her store? Although at this point she'd like to think the worst of him, Cassie shook her head. She hadn't even told him the name of her store. Well, he had deflated any romantic interest she had in him. She wasn't going to welcome Simon Legree with open arms.

Joshua had walked two blocks away from Cassie's store before excusing himself from his partner and arranging to meet him the following morning. Ken was a great business partner, even brilliant. But they'd learned long ago to let Joshua do the talking in potentially sticky situations. A perfect example was the experience with Cassie this morning. Ken didn't bother to suggest lunch, didn't even ask her name, for that matter. He just barreled through with his plans and often offended other people. Ken's IQ was intimidating, but he'd never bothered with learning much about etiquette.

Joshua turned back toward Discriminating Pleasures. He could tell his arrival had thrown Cassie. Hell, it had thrown him, too. How was he to know the best location for his business would be her store?

Pausing outside the door, he contemplated how to handle the situation. The success of his business depended on getting her to move out in time for him to open in the fall, when college started. Yet, his plans for Cassie included anything but a business relationship. He stroked his chin and shrugged his shoulders. He could only be honest, he decided as he pushed through the door.

Trying to ignore the older woman's condemning gaze as he re-entered the shop, Joshua pointed to the doors in the back. "Is Cassie's office to the left or right?"

The older woman sniffed and responded, "To the right, but I don't think she's in the mood for visitors."

He turned toward the back of the store. "Then, I guess I'd better try to change her mood."

When he entered the small, cozy office, he saw her pacing from one end of it to the other, fuming. Softly, he said, "Cassie."

She froze in midstep and turned. "What are you doing here?" She looked past him. "And where's your henchman?"

Watching her warily, Joshua shoved his hands into his pockets. "Ken's gone." He strolled around her office studying the decorative and personal touches. It was easy to see her personality in her shop and office. The scent was seductively floral, and the colors she chose ranged from pastel to vivid. Alive. She'd made this place come alive. No wonder she was angry at the thought of losing it; she'd obviously put so much of herself into the place.

Impatiently, she said, "I asked you why you're here."

Facing her, he replied, "I'm here to make sure you didn't get the wrong impression from Ken."

She crossed her arms over her chest. "And how would I get the wrong impression from Ken? Did he say anything that was incorrect?"

"No, but he didn't have to be so heartless about it." He watched her stony expression. She wasn't going to make this easy for him. "Cassie, I didn't know this was your store until I walked through your front door. This is terribly awkward for both of us."

She looked him in the eye. "Is there any possibility that you will extend my lease?"

Joshua considered hedging, but he figured he'd better go ahead and drop his bomb now. He tried to soften the blow. "We'll do everything in our power to aid you in relocating, but we need you out within two months." He watched her face fall and hurried on. "Cassie, we've studied our options and it's critical that we open at the beginning of the school semester since most of our initial business will come from the—"

Cassie cut him off and crossed her arms over her chest. "That's enough, Joshua. Perhaps I should be grateful for your honesty. But you'll have to forgive me for not feeling that way right now." Shaking her head, she continued, "I'm really not in the mood for visitors, particularly from the man who's going to kick me out of my building. So, I'd appreciate it if you'd just leave."

He considered staying to press his position, but she looked so hopeless that he decided to give her some space. Damn. The first time in years he felt such a strong pull toward a woman and he'd alienated her without even trying. He touched her arm lightly. "I'll be in touch, Cassie." With that, he turned to leave.

Watching his retreat, she sat down limply and rested her head in her hands. She almost wished he had acted nasty about buying her store. Then she'd have a better excuse for hating him. But no, he'd been reasonable and kind. She just hadn't been up to receiving any explanations. Plus, she was inordinately attracted to him. She liked his deep voice and his wavy brown hair. And when he looked at her with his intense, knowing eyes, an unexplainable thrill raced through her.

What a day! Normally, she'd consider this a great day. Several new customers stopped in, sales were brisk, but it wouldn't matter how many new customers she had if she didn't have a building for her shop. Feeling as if she were going in circles, Cassie shook her head. There must be a solution. She just hadn't thought of it.

Just then, she heard a tapping on her door. It was Kim with a pert smile on her face, which changed to concern when she saw Cassie's expression. "What's wrong? You look like somebody stole your cash register."

Cassie grimaced. "Not my cash register, but this hasn't been one of my better days." She didn't feel up to discussing her problems, so she changed the subject. "So, what brings your beaming face in here?"

"Marie and I are eating dinner at Joe's Bar and Grill tonight. We want you to come." As Cassie shook her head, Kim protested, "Aw, come on. You look like you've had a horrible day. We'll make you forget all about it." Kim grinned impishly. "Besides, if any of the guys challenge us at darts, you can leave them in the dust."

Cassie considered her friend's invitation. Perhaps it would clear some of the cobwebs from her mind if she spent some time with Kim and Marie. She was so gloomy that she knew a dinner out would help her perspective. "What time?"

"Six o'clock?"

Cassie said, "Make it six thirty, and you're on."

Kim beamed and turned to leave. "Great! We'll have a drink waiting for you."

Cassie called after her, "Make sure it's strong."

Kim waved good-bye and left. Cassie pulled a pack of crackers from her drawer and munched on them as she made plans for doing the rest of her inventory.

After she closed up shop and walked Maggie to her bus, Cassie drove home and took a shower. The shower relaxed her so that she felt like a limp noodle, and she toyed with the idea of calling Kim and cancelling. But she didn't want to hurt her friends' feelings, and her stomach was growling. Slipping on a pair of slim black jeans and a chic, cotton sweater, she wrapped her hair into a French braid and left.

She spotted Kim and Marie waving from a corner table. She sat down, noting the drink waiting for her. It looked like orange juice. Lifting it to her lips, she asked, "So, what is it?"

Marie said, "Screwdriver."

Cassie coughed, not at the taste, but at the name.

She muttered, "Well, that's keeping with the theme of my day."

"What?"

Shaking her head, Cassie replied, "Nothing." She looked around. Joe's had . . . atmosphere. The rough wood floors and tables were offset by walls decorated with nostalgic prints and advertisements. On the far side of the room, she noticed a noisy group of men playing darts. In the small lounge, a few couples danced to the sounds of Steve Winwood. The waiter approached, and the women gave them their orders.

After he left, Cassie turned to Marie. "How's everything going with your shop?" After being discontented with the manner in which her manager ran her beauty salon, Marie had recently gone out on her own.

Marie smiled. "Great. I'm so glad I followed your advice and went into business for myself." Sighing, she continued, "The hours are still pretty long, but there's nothing that compares to knowing that salon is mine, to make or break." An expression of triumph crossed her face. "And I'm making it."

Kim joked, "I'm happy for both of you lady entrepreneurs. When you two become millionaires, you can finance my business; Kim's Savings and Loan, your friendly neighborhood banker."

The three women laughed and the waiter brought their orders. While they ate their subs, they heard the dart game grow noisier and more competitive. Cassie saw the smoothly handsome blond man drawing as much attention his way as possible. He placed his back to the board and threw the dart over one shoulder, relishing the whistles. When his competitor dropped out, he complained loudly, "Is there not one worthy opponent in this establishment?'' He glanced across the room. "Hell, I'll even take on a woman at this point.''

Cassie turned away, finding him insulting and crude.

Kim nudged her. "Come on, Cassie, you gotta take this guy down a peg.''

But Cassie demurred. "It looks like a big scene, and you know how I hate those. Besides, it's not my purpose in life to change a warped personality that's been in the making for, what,'' she scrutinized him briefly, "thirty years?''

Glancing at the dart game once more, she did a double take. Who was the dark-haired guy in the jeans that fit him like God had intended jeans to fit? Then he turned and she saw his profile. Cassie groaned audibly. Hadn't she seen enough of Joshua Daniels for one day?

Marie pointed at him. "Oh, look, there's Joshua Daniels. I wonder if the other guys are here.'' Her brow knitted as she looked over the crowd. "Jack and Fred are with him,'' she said, gathering her purse. "Let's go over and join them.''

Cassie felt nonplussed. The last thing she wanted was to spend one more minute with Joshua Daniels. The man had ruined her day, her week, her month, maybe even her life. Still, she didn't want her negative feelings toward him to spill over to Kim and Marie. She smiled brightly. "You two go ahead. I'll wait for the check.''

As she stood, Kim asked, "Are you sure?'' Kim acknowledged Cassie's nod and left her money on the table. "Come over as soon as you're finished.''

Nodding vaguely, Cassie decided she would tell Kim and Marie she was leaving as soon as she paid the check. She watched them move in the direction of the men and couldn't help taking a moment to study

Joshua. She'd never seen him in casual clothing. Wearing a white pullover shirt and worn jeans that molded to his firm buttocks and strong thighs, he was a study in masculinity. The white pullover shirt revealed clearly defined pectorals, a flat abdomen, and broad shoulders. Cassie frowned. He was disgustingly sexy.

In her experience, men who were built like him were often lacking intellectually. But not Joshua. He was obviously sharp, owning his own business, completing his M.B.A., stealing her store right out from under her nose. Cassie huffed. She needed to get out of here. She couldn't deny his attractiveness. He was probably most single women's idea of a dream man. And perhaps under other circumstances . . . Well, there was no use thinking about that; she shut off her thoughts abruptly. Circumstances between Cassie and Joshua were certainly not conducive to an affair of the heart. The waiter came and Cassie paid the check.

Walking over to say good night to the girls, Cassie noticed that Joshua had joined in a discussion with the blond dart king. Cassie thought ruefully that it was difficult to decide which one she hoped would win, should they decide to play each other. In her opinion, both men could stand being taken down a peg or two. Touching Kim lightly on the shoulder, Cassie whispered, "I'm heading home, now. Thanks for inviting me."

Kim asked loudly, "What? I can't hear you."

So much for leaving quietly. Cassie enunciated clearly, "I'm going home. Thanks for inviting me."

Kim grabbed her hand. "Oh, no. You can't leave now. The game's just getting hot." She turned to the crowd. "Hey, you guys, you've got a challenger here—Cassandra Warner." The group cheered wildly.

Shaking her head at Kim, Cassie glared at her and tried to extricate herself. When she moved away, someone grabbed her hand and jerked her deeper into the crowd. The blond goon held her hand and leered at her. "Cassandra, huh? That's some sexy name. Are you sure you're ready to play with the men?"

Was he for real? Cassie was tempted to ask him where the men were, but she bit her tongue. The situation had gotten out of hand. Appalled and embarrassed, she knew her cheeks were bright red. Out of the corner of her eye, she saw Joshua studying her intently.

"My name is Blake," the blond man said. Feeling his creepy gaze run over her body, Cassie almost shivered with distaste. This was the kind of guy who could probably guess a woman's measurements to the inch, just by using his practiced eye. She crossed her arms over her chest and tapped her foot impatiently.

When he saw her look of disinterest, he raised an eyebrow. "Well, now, I think we could make this game a little more exciting with a wager."

Joshua looked down at Blake. "What kind of wager?"

"If I win the game, I get a date with Miss Cassandra here. In the unlikely event that you win, you get to take her out."

Cassie started to protest, but Joshua interrupted with a set jaw, "You're on."

She stared at him. Why in the world would he play a dart game to go out with her when they already had a date scheduled, thanks to the grocery-store contest? Then, the light dawned as she looked at both of the men. Blake strutted like a peacock, and Joshua glared at him with a frown on his face. This was some kind of macho power play with her as the pawn.

"Wait a minute. I haven't agreed to this. And besides, what if I should win?" Cassie asked them.

Blake replied smoothly, "You're not afraid of a little bet, are you?" Oozing charm, he gestured to Joshua and himself. "If you win, you get to choose between us."

Rolling her eyes, Cassie thought—*Of all the conceit, as if I would want either of them.* She bit back a sharp retort. She hadn't been the least bit interested in the dart game until this minute. Apparently, these two men needed to be taught a lesson, and for the rest of womankind, she'd have to be the one to teach it to them.

"Okay," she said mildly.

Blake cocked his head. "We don't want to overwhelm you. How about a little game of Around the Clock?"

She paused thoughtfully for a moment. "How about a little game of Killer?" she offered instead, and hid a smile at their astonished reaction. Then, thanking God for having two older brothers who would rather cheat than lose to their little sister, she was all business. "Three practice throws, one game, and no arguments."

With a look of surprise crossing their faces, the two men agreed. Joshua narrowed his eyes. Blake smiled confidently. "I don't need my practice round. You two go ahead."

This was where strategy was most important. She knew both men wanted to perform well, so she needed to lull them into a false sense of security. "It's been a while for me. I'm sure I'm a little rusty." The first one she threw barely hit the board. She heard the moans around her and bit her lip to keep from laughing. She threw the next two randomly, exhibiting the skill of a neophyte. When she finished, she offered the darts to Joshua.

His dark eyes studied her curiously as he shook his head. "I've already warmed up." He wondered what the hell she was up to. This was a different Cassie than he'd seen before. Dressed in slim black jeans and that loose sweater, she still couldn't hide her tempting curves. He'd seen her when she was flustered, charming and amusing, and angry. Now, he would see Cassie as a competitor. Something told him it would be a rare event.

Darts weren't his game. But he'd be damned if he'd let Blake get hold of Cassie. If he evaluated his feelings, he'd be totally confused. While watching Blake's heated gaze roam over her body, he experienced an overwhelming urge to punch out the guy's gleaming white teeth. He was sure that many women found Blake attractive, with his confident manner and playboy looks. Still, Cassie hadn't seemed too impressed with him. The outcome of the game would give an indication of her opinion of him. She appeared guilelessly innocent. She had something up her sleeve.

Cassie surreptitiously measured her competition. She'd selected Killer because it was the one game she won without fail whenever she played her brothers; a game that could be played with uneven players. And her brothers always got so caught up in killing each other that they forgot about her. Each player has three lives and loses one each time a dart hits his double.

"Ladies first," Joshua said.

"Okay," she moved forward and took her turn throwing a wrong-handed dart at the board to select a double. They each took turns and Cassie, with the lowest number, ended up going last.

The game progressed as she had planned. Blake exhibited his competitive streak by repeatedly aiming for Joshua's double. Fortunately, after a couple of rounds, Blake and Joshua had concentrated their energy on killing each other so that they both had only one of their three lives left, while Cassie still had two.

It was her turn, and she had to decide who to kill. She debated only momentarily, then chose Blake. After all, if something horrible happened and she didn't win, she certainly wouldn't want to end up with Blake. The very thought of it made her skin crawl. She sized up the shot, used her four-finger grip, and sent the dart whizzing perfectly into Blake's double.

Blake muttered an obscenity to which Joshua raised an eyebrow. Cassie marvelled at how effective that subtle gesture was at quelling Blake's displeasure.

Then, Joshua turned to her with a steady, intense gaze. "Your game."

She felt unsettled by the sensual warmth in his chocolate-brown eyes and took a deep breath to steady herself. Cassie pictured herself at her parents' home in the backyard. She heard her father's instructions in her mind. "Keep a steady hand, girl." Then he would laugh. "Picture the bull's-eye as the nose of someone you can't stand."

Cassie smiled, debating which face to put on the dart board. Her second throw whizzed through the air, just missing Joshua's double. She must not be concentrating hard enough.

Blocking out the jesting comments around her, she took her stance and tossed the last dart. It landed on Joshua's double. She had killed both of them and survived, leaving her the victor. She smiled benignly at her opponents, and gathered her purse to leave.

Blake protested, "Hey, you still gotta pick who you want to go out with, him or me." He smugly pointed to himself.

She looked carefully at both men, measuring each with a lengthy gaze. Blake was cocky, with his gestures and speech calculated to bring a certain response from the female half of the population. On the other hand, Joshua looked rock solid, handsome in a natural, sexy way. She could almost believe that the expression on his face hinted at uncertainty, until she remembered this afternoon. He was the man who was stealing her store.

Smiling once again, she shrugged her slender shoulders. "Neither."

With that parting statement, she turned to leave. As she pushed the bar's door open, she heard Blake blustering vehemently. Apparently his ego was hurt. She couldn't judge the condition of Joshua's pride. He was too busy laughing.

THREE

"Oh, darn!" Cassie glared at the heel that had just broken off her shoe. She had two blocks left to walk to her shop. Chewing her lip, she debated her options. She could either leave the damaged shoe on her foot and hobble lopsidedly the rest of the way, or she could remove both shoes and ruin her hose. Remembering the results of the last time she ruined her hose, she decided to hobble.

At least it wasn't raining. The glorious Carolina sky and warm temperature made her long for the sight of spring flowers. One of the disadvantages of working in downtown St. James was the lack of vegetation. Although a few of the larger companies planted some shrubs, the area was primarily concrete and brick. Cassie enjoyed flowers, so she usually kept a live or silk arrangement in her window.

Unlocking the door, Cassie turned on the lights and went to her office to retrieve the pair of sneakers she kept at the shop. The lime-green sneakers didn't exactly compliment her dress, but they would have to do. Perhaps she could pick up a new pair of shoes at lunch time.

"Good morning, Cassie." Maggie walked through the office door with a broad smile on her face.

Cassie smiled in response. "And good morning to you, Maggie. Have you heard anything about your daughter?"

Maggie simply beamed. "I sure did. She had a nine-pound boy, and my friend, Travis Beamer, is driving me up to Raleigh to visit them tomorrow."

Was Cassie mistaken or did she detect a slight blush on Maggie's face? "Sounds like this might be getting serious if Travis is interested in your grandchildren. Have you two made any plans?" Maggie, a widow for eight years, had just begun to date again. Travis was a retired postal worker who courted Maggie with flowers and bingo dates.

Sounding shocked, but acting pleased, Maggie demurred. "No, we haven't made any plans . . . yet. You'll be the first to know. Seriously, Travis is a fine man, and he treats me real nice. I wish you'd find someone nice for yourself. You don't get out enough, Cassie."

"I get out. I just don't want to get serious with anyone right now." *Or ever,* Cassie added silently. She grimaced. "As a matter-of-fact, I'm supposed to go out with someone new this weekend."

"When did this happen?" Maggie quizzed Cassie as if she expected a full report. "How come you haven't told me this before?"

And Cassie proceeded to tell Maggie the whole tale

of how she won the date with Joshua, met him at the wedding, and that he wanted them out of the building.

Maggie shook her head in dismay. "It sounds like a big mess to me. But he seemed concerned about you when he came in here the other day, and real handsome, too." Maggie chewed her gum thoughtfully. "I don't like him taking this shop away, but maybe you could talk him into letting you stay here awhile." Decisively, she said, "You oughta go out with Mr. Daniels. Besides, I bet if you think real hard you can come up with something you like about him."

Cassie didn't want to think real hard about what she liked about Joshua Daniels. That would only serve to muddy the waters. She passed off the question lightly and smiled wanly. "I beat him at darts two nights ago." Then, her smile fell. "But he's left a lot of messages on my answering machine for me to confirm the arrangements for our date. I'd love to see *Cats*. I just don't want to go with the man who's taking away my store."

Maggie clucked sympathetically, and Cassie was spared further questioning when their first customer of the day arrived.

After lunch, Cassie walked to an indoor mall two blocks from her shop. Gazing with admiration at the chic boutiques and lovely specialty shops, she wished she could move her shop to this location. There were no spaces available, however, and Cassie guessed the rents would be outrageous. After checking the mall directory, she walked toward the shoe store and stopped suddenly.

Joshua Daniels stood with a laughing, snowy-haired woman. He offered her a rose from a nearby flower stand,

and the woman kissed him on the cheek. The affection between them tugged at her heartstrings. She must be his mother, Cassie thought, as she studied the woman. The woman's eyes sparkled with adoration as she studied her son. When the woman touched his hair, Cassie saw a boyish expression cross Joshua's masculine face. Unwittingly fascinated by the tender scene, she stared. It was difficult to view Joshua as a snake in the grass when she saw him with his mother. Shaking her head once again, she turned to go.

"Cassie, I've been trying to get in touch with you."

Cassie winced when she heard Joshua's voice call after her. Ignoring his messages on her answering machine was much easier than dealing with him in person. Still, she'd appear rude if she continued to rush away. With a deep breath, she faced him and greeted him calmly. "Hello, Joshua."

"I've left several messages for you. We need to make dinner reservations, and I wanted to confirm the time with you." Joshua's dark eyes wore a skeptical expression. "Your machine isn't broken, is it?"

Feeling cornered, she backed away and said, "No, I've just been very busy. I . . . I was going to get in touch with you tonight," she lied.

"Oh," Joshua said smoothly, "then I can save you the call. Your shop closes at five, and the show starts at eight-thirty. Shall we eat at six-thirty? I could drive to your place and have the limo pick us up there at the same time."

"Limo?" she repeated weakly. She'd forgotten about the limo. Just the thought of sharing the back of a limousine with Joshua's athletic frame close to her made butterflies dance in Cassie's stomach. "Uh,

Joshua, something's come up. I don't think I'm . . ."
Her voice trailed off as the white-haired woman joined
them with a curious expression on her face.

Joshua's eyes glinted with mischief when he introduced them. "Mother, this is Cassie Warner. I've told
you all about her. We won a date at the grocery store,
and she beat me at darts the other night at Joe's."

Cassie was so mortified she could have crawled under
a rock. What must this sweet old lady think of her?
Winning a date with her son during singles' night at
the local grocery store, and then beating him at darts
at the local bar. Mustering as much dignity as possible,
Cassie extended her hand. "It's a pleasure to meet you,
Mrs. Daniels. I'm sure you're pleased that Joshua is
moving back to St. James."

Mrs. Daniels returned the handshake warmly. "Of
course, I'm thrilled that Joshua's come home. And to
see that he's already dating such a pretty girl makes me
even happier." She spoke as if she was exchanging a
confidence. "I've been wanting to see Joshua get serious with a nice girl in St. James for years."

Joshua watched Cassie's eyes widen in alarm, her
distress evident by the way her mouth opened although
no sound came out. He was accustomed to his mother's
matchmaking attempts and usually warned his dates in
advance. Cassie looked so adorably embarrassed he felt
compelled to rescue her. Placing his arm around his
mother, he admonished her, "Mother, Cassie and I
have just met. Give the woman a break." He deftly
changed the subject. "So, what brings you to the
mall?"

Relaxing visibly, Cassie answered, "I'm shopping
for shoes." When Joshua and his mother looked down

at her ratty tennis shoes, she could have cursed. What else could go wrong with this meeting? And why did she care?

Mrs. Daniel's brow wrinkled in puzzlement. "I haven't really kept up with fashion. Is this a new style?"

Cassie saw Joshua swallow an amused grin and she sighed. "No, I broke the heel of my favorite dress shoes this morning." She glanced at her watch. "Oh my, look at the time. I really must be going. My assistant will be expecting me back any minute." Cassie turned to Joshua's mother. "It was a pleasure meeting you, Mrs. Daniels, and . . . seeing you Joshua. Good—"

Breaking in, Joshua reminded her of their date. "I'll see you around six-fifteen on Saturday."

Eager to leave, she hesitated then nodded reluctantly. "Six-fifteen. Good-bye." Cassie hurried from the mall, promptly forgetting the shoes which had been the reason for her shopping trip.

Joshua watched her swift retreat and appreciated the view of her curving rear end, long legs, and bouncy hair. Yes. He could honestly say he was looking forward to getting Cassie Warner all to himself.

That evening, Cassie propped her feet up on her floral chintz sofa as she read the letter from home. She had always thought the Holly Beach newspaper could take a few lessons from her mother on keeping up with the latest news and gossip in the area. The purpose of this letter was to remind Cassie of the annual family reunion being held in a few weeks at her parents' home.

Her older brothers, Ben and Ross, would be there. Apparently Ross's wife, Darlene, wouldn't be eating much since she was presently in the throes of morning sickness with her third pregnancy. Cassie smiled as she thought of how Ross had changed with marriage and fatherhood. He used to have the reputation of a devil until Darlene came along and tamed him. Whenever Darlene became pregnant, Ross was solicitous of every move she made. Ben, however, remained as free as a bird. Leaning on his high school and college sports experience, Ben had become an athletic equipment sales representative, travelling throughout the southeast. Cassie rolled her eyes in amusement. He probably had a girl in every town.

Cassie read on to discover that her mother had slipped in one disturbing piece of information. Apparently, Billy Joe Hart had left his second wife and was in the process of divorce. He'd called her mother several times asking for Cassie's address and phone number. Groaning, Cassie remembered the last time Billy Joe had gotten a divorce. He'd played on every one of Cassie's emotions to get her to see him again.

"Aw, come on, Cassie," Billy Joe had said, "I shouldn't have ever married Sheila, and you know it. You're not gonna punish me forever just because of one mistake, are you?"

Cassie sighed in response. "For the last time, I'm not punishing you. Things just aren't the same between us anymore." She lifted her palms in exasperation. "I don't even live in Holly Beach."

"You could move back here. Don't you remember how good everything was between us?" Billy Joe took her into his arms and kissed her seductively.

Cassie had pulled away and taken a long, hard look at Billy Joe Hart. She used to think the sun rose and set on him, with his blond hair and blue eyes. She remembered how she practically shrieked for joy when he proposed to her when she was nineteen. But his handsome face didn't take her breath away anymore. The lips that had once appeared so sensual to her now seemed weak. The voice that had once sounded boyishly expressive now whined. Yes, he was still handsome in a pretty way. But Cassie saw now what a star struck nineteen year old could not see. Billy Joe lacked strength and staying power.

One month before their scheduled wedding, after Billy Joe's constant wheedling, they made love in the backseat of his car. He hadn't touched her again after that night, and she'd been too embarrassed and insecure to ask him why. Later, she discovered that he was still playing the high-school stud. He'd gotten another girl pregnant before their engagement. The terrified pregnant teenager had confronted him with the news the day after Billy Joe and Cassie had consumated their relationship.

He had waited until the last minute, hoping the other girl would terminate the pregnancy. When she wouldn't, he eloped with her and dumped the responsibility for cancelling the wedding arrangements on Cassie.

Anger had ripped through her—at Billy Joe, at herself. How could she have been so blind? Her anger had given her the courage to speak. "Billy Joe, whatever was between us was over a long time ago. I'm different now. I really hope you find what you're looking for, but it's not me. Don't ever ask me again."

Sullenness replaced sensuality on his face. "You're just mad because I left you at the altar. It's your loss, now. We could have been good together."

Cassie had watched him stiffly walk away and felt

only relief. She'd always found it difficult to refuse Billy Joe until now. Now, she felt free. She was over him.

The timer on the microwave broke her reverie and she rose to eat her dinner. She'd gotten over Billy Joe Hart a long time ago. And she'd never gotten serious with another man. Oh, sure, she had more than her share of dates and friends. Lifting the top off the diet dinner to allow it to cool, Cassie wondered when she would ever get serious again.

Her thoughts drifted to Joshua: his strong face and laughing brown eyes. She was very attracted to Joshua, but she couldn't see how a relationship with him would ultimately bring anything but pain. After all, he was going to kick her out of his building. And Cassie couldn't dismiss that little fact because her store meant too much to her.

Sitting on her sofa, Cassie crossed her legs and checked the time again. He was late. A mere ten minutes, but it was enough to make her edgy. What if he didn't come? Should she call the restaurant to let them know they'd be late? And what should she do about that mile-long white limousine parked at her front door?

Abandoning her seat on the sofa, Cassie stood and paced the length of her small living room, cursing men in general and lamenting her fateful visit to the grocery store over a week ago. Although she hadn't wanted to admit it, Cassie was looking forward to this date with Joshua. She had taken extra care with her appearance; selecting a feminine soft blue dress with billowy short sleeves, dropped waist, and a pleated hem that teased her upper calves. She paired it with matching earrings and white, strappy sandals.

Finding his business card with that of his partner's left on her desk this morning had thrown her momentarily. Apparently, they had taken her advice and used their own key to visit her store during non-business hours. A sense of dread had settled within her. Her impressions of Joshua were confused. If only he wasn't making her move her store.

Cassie was trying to decide whether to tell the limo driver to leave or to go on without Joshua when her doorbell rang. Catching her breath, she forced an outward expression of calm and opened the door.

Before she completely opened the door, Joshua said, "Cassie, I'm sorry I'm late. I've had a little family emergency this afternoon and—" He paused and stared at her. "God, you're gorgeous."

The warmth of his admiring gaze washed over her, and Cassie felt the responding tingle within. She could have forgiven him far more than fifteen minutes' tardiness at that point and easily returned the compliment. He wore a black, chalk-striped suit with a cream shirt and burgundy tie, and his hair was slightly mussed, as if he'd been running his fingers through it. When he reached his hand to his hair, she smiled at her accuracy. She turned to get her bag. "Is it your mother? She's not ill, is she?"

Shaking his head, Joshua's face tightened as he took her arm and replied, "No, it's a, uh, distant relative." He helped her into the car and asked, "How was business today?"

Cassie stiffened at his mention of the store. It was a sore subject between them, but if he wanted to raise the issue, she'd let him know where she stood. "Steady. A lot of people come downtown in the spring and summer for their shopping." She cleared her throat. "Joshua, I've asked you once, but for the sake of my business, I must ask you again. Is there any possible way you can give me an extension on my lease? I may lose my business because I can't find a location soon enough. Is it so important that you start up in two months?"

"Yes, it is so important that I open in two months," he answered impatiently.

At his curt response, Cassie sat back and laced her fingers together, carefully studying her pink naïl polish.

Joshua observed her defensive posture and sighed, realizing he'd alienated her with his sharp retort. He reached for her hands, which she reluctantly allowed him to hold between his own. "Cassie, I'd give anything if you weren't the tenant in my building. But the fact remains that you are, and I need you out before the end of your lease, if possible. I don't think I can explain to you how important the success of this particular store is to me." He stopped abruptly, seemingly uncomfortable with what he had revealed.

"I know you don't like it that I'm not renewing your lease, but I've been looking forward to going out with you the whole week. Do you think we could set aside our differences on the subject, just for this evening?"

When she remained quiet, he smiled engagingly. "So far, I know you can dance, run fast, leave me in the dust with darts, and you're beautiful. I'd like to know more, and I know your gift shop is important to you. So, how about if we start there?"

Under the onslaught of his masculine appeal, Cassie felt herself bend a little. She promised herself she'd pursue this issue with him at another time. She smiled reluctantly and realized she wanted to put their barriers aside for the evening, also. The limousine created a friendly, intimate atmosphere and she proceeded to tell him about some of her more eccentric customers. He listened and responded, and Cassie found herself enjoying his undivided attention.

The French restaurant where they dined offered exquisite service and food. They laughed over each other's dismal French and shared remembrances of their high school experiences with foreign languages. No sooner had they finished their dessert before they were whisked away to the St. James Theatrical Auditorium.

Although Cassie thoroughly enjoyed the musical, she was more aware of Joshua's presence beside her. At some point during the show, he rested his arm on the back of her chair, making her appreciate his long, lean build and enticing masculine scent.

Laughing at the antics of the cats, she felt him squeeze her shoulder and turned to him. The amusement in his eyes was replaced with a look of such intense longing that Cassie caught her breath. His eyes roamed over her face and hair, and he moved his hand to cup the honeyed hair at her nape. His gaze ensnared hers and he moved forward to kiss her. Pleasure thrummed through her at his stroking fingers and Cassie leaned into his touch. Her heart raced when his mouth hovered less than a breath from her lips. Suddenly, the auditorium lights came on. The play was over. With an expression of regret, Joshua kissed her lightly on the forehead and released her.

He checked his watch and a worried expression came

over his face. "I need to make a quick phone call. Would you wait for me?"

Still dazed from their momentary intimacy, Cassie nodded. "Of course, I'll meet you in the lobby." She watched him go and wondered again what was bothering him.

After making a trip to the ladies' room to brush her hair and freshen her lipstick, Cassie sat on a bench waiting for Joshua. He strode toward her with a grim expression on his face.

"Once again, Cassie, I'm sorry, but I'm going to have to let you take the limo home by yourself. Something's come up and I have to take care of it immediately," Joshua said tightly.

Her heart filled with compassion at the bleakness in his brown eyes. "Joshua, can't you tell me what's wrong?"

His face closed up at her inquiry. "It's a family matter. Nothing to concern yourself with."

Hurt by his cold manner, she turned away. "I didn't mean to pry."

He stared at her briefly and then looked away, as if the words were painful to say. "I'm adopted." He sighed and sat down beside her. "The Daniels adopted me when I was five years old. Social Services had my natural father declared unfit, and I was living in a foster home. My natural mother died when I was born. Originally, the Daniels had planned on adopting an infant, but they wanted me after they met me." Joshua laughed dryly. "Guess it was my natural charm. The day they took me home was the happiest day of my life. They've been great parents in a less-than-perfect situation."

Joshua's smile fell. "My natural father is the family

emergency. He's an alcoholic rambler. He likes to come around every once in a while to remind me of where I came from." Sighing again, he continued, "He always phones my mother to find out where I am, and it upsets her."

Something inside her ripped wide open at the image of a young Joshua struggling to deal with all the changes he'd been through. Deeply affected by his story, Cassie hardly knew how to respond. She only knew that for some reason she didn't want Joshua left alone to deal with this painful situation. Covering his hand lightly with hers, she asked, "Where is he? What do you need to do?"

Twining his fingers within hers, Joshua turned to her. "He's about to get thrown out of a bar two blocks away from here. I'll go pay for a hotel room for him for the night and have room service bring him breakfast in the morning. I'll try to get him to commit himself to a treatment center, but he won't. He'll sleep off his drink and be gone tomorrow." He dropped her hand and framed her face with his fingers. "Listen, Cassie, you've been great. But I've gotta get him taken care of before they throw him into jail. Let me walk you out to the limo." He smiled sadly. "Believe me, I hate that our date has to end this way."

"Well, it's not going to," Cassie blurted out and wondered at her impulsiveness. "The limousine is at our disposal all night. We'll drive to that bar and take your father to a hotel, and then go finish up the rest of the Rocky Road ice cream in my freezer."

Joshua laughed and stroked her cheek. "Ah, Cassie, I had this feeling about you the first time I saw you. I appreciate the offer, but I can't let you do it. My father's not exactly a pretty sight when he's drunk. I need to get you home.''

They argued back and forth, with Joshua becoming more adamant with each exchange.

Finally, Cassie pulled out all the stops. ''Are you saying you don't like Rocky Road ice cream?'' With an exaggerated sigh, she said, ''Well, I guess if you're going to be picky about it, we can stop at an all-night grocery store.''

She turned serious and stood. ''Come on, Joshua, I can wait in the limo while you take care of him. Let's go.'' When she saw that he was about to protest, she threatened, ''I beat you at darts, so you owe me. And I'm collecting now.''

Snatching her hand, Joshua pulled her back to him. He ran a thumb lightly over her bottom lip. ''This is against my better judgment,'' he muttered, ''but I don't have time to argue with a mule-headed female right now.''

They walked to the waiting limousine and rode the two blocks to the bar. After getting out of the car, Joshua assured Cassie that he wouldn't be long.

The smoke in the rundown bar was so thick you could cut it with a knife. Joshua coughed. Or choked on it. Setting his jaw grimly, he searched the faces for that of his father. Dear old dad always seemed to pick the seediest places in town. Joshua heard his name rasped out by an elderly man who seemed to be holding on to the wall for balance. He studied the man intently. Wearing tattered, soiled clothes and with a gray-whiskered face, the man resembled a bum. His bottle was wrapped in a paper bag. And as Joshua came closer, he saw that the man's eyes were vacant and bloodshot. "Harry?"

The old man's eyes clouded in confusion, then cleared. "Harry, yeah, that's me, Harry. Hello, son. It's good to see you. It's been such a long time," Harry said in slurred tones, and raised his voice. "Hey, everybody, this is my son, Joshua. He's a big-shot college graduate. Ain't it hard to believe he started out with me?"

Joshua struggled with the familiar shame and embarrassment. The surrounding people glanced over disinterestedly and turned away. When Harry began laughing uncontrollably, Joshua knew it was time to coax the man to the hotel room. Having been through this scenario a few times before, Joshua had learned when his father was close to collapsing. "Come on, Harry, I've got a room with your name on it. You can sleep off this bottle and they'll give you breakfast in the morning."

Moving his head negatively, he replied. "No, don't want any food. My stomach doesn't feel too good. I could use some money, though."

Then, with only a weak protest, Harry complied when Joshua took the older man's arm and led him out of the bar. Thankfully, the bar was underneath a hotel, so they didn't have far to go. Compensating for Harry's drunken movements by placing one arm around the old man's back, Joshua led his father to the front desk and secured a room for the night.

By the time they made it to the hotel room, the old man was hanging limply in Joshua's arms. Picking up his father, he carried him to the bed and laid him down. Harry had a death grip on the bottle, and Joshua had to pry his fingers away from it, one by one. Joshua turned his head and sat silently for a moment, steeling himself against the barrage of emotions that hit him.

Methodically, he walked to the bathroom and poured the liquor down the drain, chasing it with water from the tap to rid the bathroom of the overwhelming odor. Following his routine, Joshua dampened a washcloth and went back to Harry. After removing his father's jacket, he loosened the clothing and removed the hole-ridden shoes. He gently wiped his father's face and neck with the damp washcloth.

Harry stirred. "You're a good boy, Joshua. Your dad would be proud to see you."

Joshua frowned in confusion. Then he realized that the alcohol had muddled his father's mind. "You can change, Harry. There are people specially trained to help you. I'll leave a phone number, and you can call them in the morning."

"Yeah," mumbled Harry, "in the morning."

Sighing, Joshua took the washcloth back to the bathroom and filled a glass with water to put on the nightstand. He looked at his drunken father once more and murmured, "Good night, Harry." Then he left the room.

The familiar shaking overtook Joshua when he was halfway down the hall. He hadn't cried over his father's drunkenness since he was five years old. But every time after he got his father a hotel room and carried him to it, Joshua got the shakes. Taking a deep breath, he stopped and berated himself as he leaned against the wall. *You'd think I'd be used to this, that it wouldn't affect me at all.* Still, something about the sight of his father, poisoned by his addiction to alcohol, overwhelmed Joshua every time. Harry's emaciated form and spoiled clothing ripped at his emotions. Although Joshua had stopped viewing Harry as a father figure years ago, he anguished over the complete waste of human life.

At least this time, Cassie was waiting for him with her plans for ice cream. Smiling at the thought of her, Joshua felt the shaking subside and continued down the hall. Cassie. She had no idea what a source of healing she represented to him tonight.

He stopped by the front desk and arranged for a light breakfast to be sent to Harry's room the next morning. Then he walked to the limousine and climbed inside.

She searched his implacable face carefully, but remained silent. She sensed his mind was still with his father and she wanted to give him the space he needed.

After a few minutes, she gently prodded him. "Is he okay?"

He nodded.

"How about you?"

"I'm fine," he said in a quiet voice.

Smiling tentatively, she said, "Then I guess we'd better discuss ice cream since you don't like Rocky Road."

His heart turned over at her charm and Joshua wrapped an arm around her slender shoulders.

After a good natured argument over ice cream flavors, they wound up back at Cassie's house with bowls of Rocky Road ice cream and raspberry sherbet, respectively. Watching Joshua finish up two bowls, she felt a measure of satisfaction in diverting his attention from his father. Joshua looked relaxed, comfortable, and far too sexy for this time of night. He'd removed his coat, loosened his tie, and pushed up his shirt sleeves. His tousled brown hair made her fingers itch to run through it, and his shirt and slacks fit his body in a very distracting way.

Earlier, Cassie had viewed Joshua as a friend in need of another caring human being, and she'd been happy to play the part. But now, Joshua Daniels seemed like a large man taking up a large part of her sofa and an even larger space in her mind. If there was one thing she'd learned about him this evening, it was that he had the potential to be very disturbing to her peace of mind. Therefore, there would be no more dates, she decided. Now, she just had to let him know that.

"Ah, Cassie, this has been great." He looked at her bowl. "You finished? Let me take that into the kitchen."

She watched him make himself at home and felt a tinge of uneasiness. When he came back into the living room, he sat close to her and stretched his arm behind her shoulders. His eyes were sleepy and warm, and she felt a tightening in her throat as he drew her to him.

"When can we do this again?" He moved closer and their breaths mingled with the scents of raspberry and chocolate. "Next time, it'll be just you and me, without any interruptions."

His mouth was temptation itself and with an enormous effort, she pulled back. "Joshua," she said huskily. "I don't think this is a good idea."

His arms locked around her and his eyes deepened with sensual intent. He blew a wisp of hair from her forehead. "What's not a good idea?"

Her heart thumped wildly. "Uh, you kissing me. I think—"

He interrupted. "I think I'm past thinking."

He pressed his warm mouth on Cassie's and she knew she should stop him, but the feelings he aroused in her were too rare and delicious.

His tongue teased the corner of her mouth, and without forethought Cassie opened her lips to his gentle probes. Joshua's embrace tightened, bringing her silk-covered breasts into contact with his hard chest. The friction of his cotton shirt against the soft material of her dress made a sensual sound. A wispy sigh escaped her lips as his tongue explored the recesses.

His fingers stroked her ribs, and she twined her arms around his neck and leaned into his warmth and strength. Her movement inflamed him, and he groaned and ran his hands on the outer curves of her breasts while his avid mouth deliberately provoked her response.

The breath seemed to stop in her throat. Their kisses were both physical and emotional, drawing on the events of the evening. A bond had formed between them, urging her closer to him even as she knew she should pull back.

He released her mouth slowly, stealing little kisses from the corners of her lips. He whispered against her forehead, "Oh, God, Cassie, you're so sweet."

The brief respite from his mouth brought her a sliver of consciousness, and Cassie flushed at her body's betrayal. "Oh, my," she exclaimed softly.

Lifting her chin with an index finger, Joshua studied her passion-tinted face. Her aqua eyes were dark with arousal, her lips rosy from his kisses, and he found her wholly desirable. His own arousal made him painfully aware that he probably had a cold shower ahead of him.

He'd gotten carried away, and he knew with certainty he'd welcome the opportunity to finish what they had started. Seeing confusion and embarrassment steal across her face, he knew he'd better do something fast or he would lose any rapport he'd gained with her tonight.

Clearing his throat, he thrust aside the desire to ravish her and reluctantly released her. He raked his fingers through his hair and said, "Uh, I didn't intend to keep you out so late after a full work day. I'm sure we're both tired. I'd like to see you again." Joshua saw the protest form on her lips and spoke quickly. "I'm in a real bind. I've promised to take the kids at church tubing on the St. James river and I don't have enough chaperones. I'd really appreciate it if you could help out."

Caught off guard, Cassie stared at him without answering. After his sensual kiss, she'd expected just about anything but a request to help chaperone kids for a tubing trip. She was confused, then she gave a laugh of relief.

Seeing that he was waiting for a response, she replied uncertainly. "I haven't been tubing since I was in college. I don't—"

With a boyish smile, Joshua broke in, "Oh, that's no problem. Tubing's like riding a bike. You never forget." He stood and continued, "We're going tomorrow afternoon around two-thirty. I'll pick you up around one-thirty, okay?"

"I guess."

Catching her hand and squeezing it, he said. "Great, I'll see you tomorrow." He walked to the door and over his shoulder, he said, "Thanks again for tonight, Cassie."

And Cassie sat on her sofa staring after him blankly, wondering how she'd gotten herself committed to seeing him again.

FOUR

"Would you mind putting some of this sunscreen on my back, Cassie?"

Staring dumbly at the bottle Joshua thrust into her hand, she wondered again what had possessed her to come on this tubing expedition with him. The group designated this picnic area as the meeting place, and Cassie and Joshua had just arrived to wait for the rest of the crowd.

Even though Joshua had opened the car door to his silver Trans Am, Cassie still felt a bit claustrophobic. She watched him pull his T-shirt over his head and swallowed at the sight of his broad shoulders and muscular back. And she was supposed to touch his skin?

Joshua grinned at her over his shoulder. "Earth to Cassie. Come in. I'd do it myself, but you can reach it better than I can."

His teasing brought her back and she took a fortifying breath. For Pete's sake, it's just a back. A gorgeous back, but . . . Cassie flipped off the top and squirted the cream into her hand. Not bothering to rub her hands together, she briskly slapped it onto his back.

Joshua arched his back and winced. "Where'd you take masseuse lessons, the Antarctic?"

Serves him right, she thought caustically. The combination of her cold, nervous hands and the cold lotion had shocked him. It was reassuring to know that she wasn't the only uncomfortable one. Muttering an apology, she proceeded to rub the cream into his smooth skin, appreciating the firm muscles.

Her hands warmed quickly over Joshua's slick skin, moving over his shoulders, down his spine, and finally to the top of his denim cut-offs. She couldn't help but admire his tight buttocks. And by the time she finished the job, Cassie felt warm all over from Joshua's approving murmurs and the rippling of his muscles. "All done," she said weakly.

Turning around to face her, Joshua's eyes darkened with desire and the atmosphere in the car seemed to thicken.

He caught her hand and leaned closer to her, speaking in a husky voice, "Can I return the favor?"

Feeling his breath on her lips, Cassie nearly gave into the sensual pull of his eyes. Just as she leaned the rest of the way forward, a horn sounded and she drew a quick breath in her retreat.

"No, if you want to do me a favor, you can extend my lease." She reached for her bag and pushed open the door. She desperately needed to get out of that car, away from Joshua. Lord, letting that man close to her was guaranteed to put her brain into automatic shut-down. Although she felt his curious gaze upon her, she refused to look at him and called out to Kim and Fred.

"Cassie," Kim called. "I didn't know you were coming. How'd you get roped into chaperoning our tubing expedition?"

Cassie smiled wryly in response. "I haven't figured that out yet." When she saw Kim's puzzled brow, she continued, "So, what's the plan? How many kids are coming?"

"We've got about thirty kids. Their parents are dropping them off here and meeting us downstream in three hours." Kim grinned mockingly at a carload of teenagers pulling into the picnic area. "Here come some of the darlings now." Turning back to Cassie, Kim said, "Seriously, Cassie, I'm glad you could come. We were a little edgy about not having enough adults."

At that moment, Joshua stepped behind her and rested his hand on her shoulder. Jerking her head around, she noticed his sneaky smile as he murmured, "Yeah, I'd say we've all been a little edgy, haven't we, Cassie?"

Edgy was putting it mildly. Cassie was certain the heat from his gaze would have burned steel. She moved away from him and forced her eyes away from the arresting picture his bare chest made. Funny how she could look at Fred's chest without a flicker of response, but she couldn't look at Joshua without feeling flushed and overheated.

Another car arrived with more teenagers and a tall, short-haired blonde woman who Cassie almost mistook for one of the kids.

"Oh, there's Tricia." Kim explained to Cassie, "She's the church youth director. A real sweetheart."

Then Kim lowered her voice. "Better watch out, though, I hear she's got a mile-wide crush on Joshua."

Cassie was about to protest, then changed her mind. Tricia was tall and slim with an engaging smile, and Cassie didn't like the odd mix of feelings she experienced when she watched the young woman lay her hand on Joshua's arm and lean into him as they shared a chuckle. Jealousy had no place in a platonic relationship, and that's what she wanted with him.

Tricia called everyone to attention and deferentially asked Joshua to go over the safety rules. When he finished, the kids grabbed the inner tubes and raced to the river.

Cassie saw Joshua moving in her direction and those uneasy feelings began to surface within her, so she waved her hand at him as she snatched an inner tube. "See ya down river, Joshua. Gotta catch up with the kids." She felt a bit cowardly about running out on him, but justified her actions by reasoning that she was there to chaperone.

Growling in frustration, Joshua placed his hands on his hips and stared after the elusive woman who had occupied his mind so much lately. Damn. The lady's as slippery as an eel.

She made a lovely picture floating in the water with a delighted smile on her face, with her long legs stretched over the edge of the inner tube, her honey hair damp and tossed. She wore old cut-offs and a T-shirt that was plastered over, he looked more closely, a blue bathing suit. In Joshua's eyes, she was sexy personified, and he wanted her with an intensity that was beginning to drive him mad. Remembering his responsibility to chaperone the kids, he watched the last few enter the water and followed after them.

Spinning down the river, Cassie gripped her tube tightly and laughed when the water sloshed into her face. She reminded the kids to stay away from the rocks, recalling several times in her college days when she'd ripped her shorts on the sharp rocks. She hadn't been able to sit down comfortably for days.

Cassie watched the kids coast down the river and held back to see if there were any more from her group. Then, Cassie heard a cry of distress. She narrowed her eyes, searching all around for the sound. What she saw sent her heart into her throat. A couple with two young children had tied their tubes together to splash around in a calm pool next to the banks of the river.

Apparently, they'd wandered farther from the edge than they intended. The youngster had slipped from his inner tube and was being swallowed by the currents.

Not wasting a moment of time, Cassie abandoned her own inner tube and raced through the water with powerful strokes. The little boy wore a life vest, but he couldn't keep his head above the water. She kept her eyes on the bobbing orange vest and tried not to think about the sharp rocks.

While the distraught mother held the other child, the father called out in a loud voice. "Timmy, hold on! I'm coming!"

But the current frustrated his efforts.

Recalling her swim teacher's instructions, Cassie swam alongside the current instead of against it. Finally, the bobbing life jacket was just inches from her fingers. Stretching with all her might, she reached and felt the fabric between her fingers, only to have it slip away.

Vaguely hearing the distressed voices of the little boy's parents, she pushed away her panic and kicked forward once again. With both hands this time, she reached and held the jacket in a death grip.

Gazing down at the preschooler, her heart fell. He was too quiet. He should be screaming, choking, or gasping. Adrenaline coursed through her bloodstream. She pulled the boy into a small cove and pushed off his life vest. By this time, his father had arrived by her side.

Cassie's attention remained on the child. Red hair, freckles on a pug nose, and blue lips.

"What's wrong? Oh, God. He's not breathing. He's not breathing!" the man practically sobbed. He ran his hands over Timmy.

"Then we'll just have to make him breathe again," she muttered with determination and placed the boy on his back on the ground.

"Do you know CPR?" the man asked her. He pulled her arm. "Please tell me you do."

"It might not come to that." Cassie cupped the back of Timmy's head. Then she pinched his nose and blew a puff into his mouth. She automatically breathed into his little mouth at five-second intervals several more times, and a wonderful thing happened. Timmy spit out the river water he'd swallowed, coughing and gasping.

When he'd finished, he stared up with wide, blue eyes at Cassie. Then he squished his eyes together and wailed loudly. "Mo-o-mmy," he called and began sobbing.

Relief surged through her and she felt her hand

clasped by his father. "I can't thank you enough." He released her and grabbed his son to his chest. "Oh, Timmy. You scared us to death."

Timmy continued to cry; he still wanted his mother. The man stood, holding Timmy tightly in his arms. He turned to Cassie, his cheeks wet from tears. "How can I thank you?"

Cassie's heart went out to him. The couple had obviously planned a day of family fun and almost lost something very precious in the process. She patted the youngster's head. "Anyone would have done the same thing. I was just nearby at the time."

"But you cut through those currents when I couldn't."

Cassie gave a faint smile. "I lived on the beach until five years ago. I've got a lot of experience with those currents." She grew serious. "I'm sure I don't have to tell you this now, but you might want to stick to pools and lakes until this one gets a little older."

The man shook his red head, and Cassie noticed the strong resemblance between him and Timmy. He released a shaky breath. "It'll be a while before we graduate past the bathtub and kiddie pools." He shifted Timmy and extended his hand to her. "I'm Paul McCoy. If you think of a way we can repay you, we're in the St. James phone book."

"Cassie Warner," she returned the introduction and the handshake. "It's thanks enough that Timmy's okay."

They both heard the voice of Timmy's mother calling. Paul gave her a shaky smile and walked along the edge of the river. "Ellen," he yelled. "Timmy's fine."

Breathing a sigh, Cassie collapsed on the ground and clasped her head between her hands. Although the entire rescue had taken under five minutes, it had seemed forever. When she'd agreed to chaperone a bunch of teenagers, she'd never expected something like this happening.

She needed a moment to gather her wits, she told herself. The sight of that limp little boy gave her shivers.

Her T-shirt was soaked and clinging, so she pulled it off for a few minutes. The warmth of the afternoon sun felt wonderful on her cool, wet body and she closed her eyes in search of contentment. After lying that way for a few moments, she realized she should rejoin the group before she was missed.

Just as she sat up, she saw Joshua moving toward her with a determined glint in his eye and a purposefulness in his gait. At that moment, Cassie realized that she had underestimated Joshua in a fatal way. Without his clothing, he was stripped of his civilized veneer. His upper body muscles and his biceps were just this side of bulky, and his powerful legs revealed a man well-acquainted with physical activity. The mat of dark brown hair covering his chest disappeared into wet, brief cut-offs that clung mercilessly to his masculine form. Cassie swallowed at his imposing physique.

Joshua stopped within inches of her and regarded her with a curious gaze. "I ran into some guy with a red-haired kid. He was babbling something about how his son almost drowned. He said a lady named Cassie had rescued Timmy." He sat down beside her. "Do you mind telling me what happened?"

When he sat down, she shrugged and scooted over. "It wasn't that bad. I just came over here to catch my breath." Cassie's eyes scanned the river. "Where are

Tricia and the others?'' Not giving him a chance to answer, she began to stand. "I'm really much better now. I think I'm ready to—"

He pulled her down on his lap and demurred, "Oh, no, you don't. You've been running since we first started this field trip. Look at you," he said with concern. "You're trembling."

Uncomfortably aware of her skin pressed against his, Cassie protested. "Joshua, we're supposed to be chaperoning the kids. What if one of them gets hurt? I'll tell you about it later."

Joshua merely shook his head. "No way. We talk now. The teenagers were having a contest for who could drink the most lemonade when I left." He rubbed his hands up and down her arms to warm them.

"It was scary," she admitted, relaxing against his solid body. "I guess he took in too much water. He wasn't breathing when I caught up with him." She shuddered.

Sensing her distress, he wrapped his arms more tightly around her. "His parents should have been more careful. How'd he get away from them?"

His lips rubbed against her forehead. The gesture of comfort sent spirals of warmth throughout her body. Cassie shook her head. "It was just an accident. I don't think they'll be bringing their kids tubing for a long time. The father was pretty shaken up about it."

"Are you okay?" His voice rumbled deliciously against her ear.

She nodded.

"You were brave." He scattered kisses along her cheek and eyes.

Cassie knew she should move, but the spell he cast

over her made her knees weak. "I don't think I'm cut out for being a lifeguard," she whispered.

"You don't like mouth-to-mouth contact?" He stopped her efforts to answer the question with a deep, wet kiss.

She fought the languidness stealing over her. "Joshua," she protested, "we don't need this with the store between us. You must feel the same way—"

He cut her off with a movement so swift she felt dizzy. Joshua had her flat on her back beneath him. His eyes roamed hungrily over her sun-tinted face. "I want to clear up any illusions you may have about my feelings for you."

When Cassie realized his intent, she squirmed against him and shook her head in denial. But Joshua was determined and his mouth descended on hers, stealing her breath. Cassie held her mouth in rigid mutiny. Yet, he chipped away at her resistance by nibbling and sucking on her lips. His avid mouth teased and tempted her until, with a sigh, she surrendered and gave the response he sought.

Her hands stole around his neck and she dug her fingers into his damp hair. A burning sensation licked through her veins when he thrust his tongue into her mouth eliciting her heated participation. Their tongues thrust and parried in a wild dance mimicking a more intimate ritual, and she was intoxicated with the lemony, raw male taste of him.

When his mouth left hers to trail a string of kisses against her neck, she heard him mutter, "Woman, you're driving me mad." She gasped as he flicked his tongue over her ear.

"You taste like honey and feel like heaven."

His rough voice skittered across her sensitive skin like a stone skipping across water, drawing her deeper into the maelstrom of his desire.

He traced the border of her bathing suit with his finger, then reached down to brush his thumb over the peak of her breast. Feeling the tension within her increase to a fever pitch, Cassie arched her body against his.

Her movement tested his control and he returned to kiss her mouth with almost savage intensity. He quickly pushed down the straps of her bathing suit, baring her breasts to him.

Raising himself slightly above her, his glazed eyes took in her womanly mounds. His breath caught in his throat at the sight of her beauty; her hooded eyes and tousled hair, passion-swollen lips, her creamy skin and the already tight tips of her breasts, which seemed to beckon and tempt him. Groaning, he surrendered to the temptation and took her precious rosiness into his mouth.

Cassie whimpered at the friction of his adoring tongue on her tender nipples. She'd never experienced this heat and passion. Her experience with Billy Joe had been rushed, leaving her with a vague dissatisfaction. But, this was . . . Oh, God, she didn't know how much more of his ministrations she could stand. The burning ache Joshua started within her threatened to enflame her. Her sanity gone the way of the wind, Cassie writhed beneath him.

Joshua had intended only to kiss her, but at the first touch of her lips, he'd been unable to stop. And those hungry, passionate sounds she made were driving him wild. He was aroused to the point of pain, and as she twisted her body restlessly against him, he brought his mouth back to hers.

He drove his tongue deep into her mouth, and Cassie gloried in the feel of his hard chest crushing her breasts. Her passion drove everything but Joshua from her mind. Her senses were filled only with him; the taste of him, the sensation of his hard body pressed against her, and the desire to get closer to him. Circling his tongue with her own, she fought to continue the kiss even as her lungs demanded air. They broke apart only briefly to inhale quickly, then merged their slick mouths back together.

Cassie felt his hard masculinity press against that part of her that ached for him so. His strong legs nudged her thighs apart and she instinctively lifted her hips in response to the thrust of his body against hers. The wild tempo increased and Cassie murmured, "Oh, Joshua."

Then, suddenly she no longer felt the weight of his warm body. The sun shone brightly in her eyes and with an overwhelming sense of confusion she looked to her side and found Joshua gasping for breath with his head locked in his hands.

Her body felt like an instrument that had played a beautiful song only to have the music abruptly cut off, without resolution. The sounds of the real world penetrated her sensual daze.

Glancing down at her naked breasts, Cassie made a muffled sound of dismay and struggled to cover herself. She'd wanted him to finish what he'd started with her. The passion still coursed through her veins making her hands shake. She would have let this man take her on the side of a river while they were supposed to be chaperoning teenagers. The incongruity of the situation baffled her.

Her embarrassment was made even more acute by the knowledge that he had been the one to stop this insanity and not her. She felt his gaze on her, but couldn't look at him. And she couldn't exactly protest and act offended when she'd matched his ardor with her own. Just how does a woman act after she's practically given herself to a man she had every intention of discouraging?

Watching Cassie's awkward movements, Joshua averted his face and groaned inwardly. *Great job, stud,* he berated himself. They'd both gotten a little carried away and he could tell that she probably thought it was the end of the world. A little carried away. Ha! One wouldn't say that by how tight his cut-offs still were. If he hadn't heard the distant sound of frolicking teenagers, God knows what would have happened. He needed to find a way to cool them both off and add a little levity to the situation.

Joshua eyed the river and shrugged. Why fight nature?

Reaching over to Cassie, he hauled her up into his arms and ran into the water.

"Oh! What are you doing?" Cassie screamed as he dumped her into the river. She emerged gasping and glared at him. "You could have warned me."

"Why? So you could argue about it?" Joshua shook his head, intentionally spraying her with the moisture from his hair. "I sure as hell needed cooling off, and I figured it wouldn't hurt you any either. What are you staring at?"

With an amused grin, she pointed at his head.

"What? What's on my head?" Joshua asked as he ran his fingers through his hair.

"It's your hair. You've got more cowlicks than Dennis the Menace." She tried unsuccessfully to control her mirth at the sight of his hair spiked out in every direction. "You'd fit in real well with the kids' styles, if you dyed it pink or green."

"Oh, yeah. So you like my hairstyle, huh?" Joshua grabbed her shoulders and glared at her with mock indignation. "It looks like we need to do something to yours. I wouldn't want you to feel left out." He grinned at her shriek as he rubbed furiously at her hair, pulling it in front of her eyes.

Releasing her suddenly, he said, "There, I'd say we're about even now."

They were acting like a couple of kids playing in the water, and Cassie wondered where her discomfort and embarrassment had gone. She groaned and ducked her head under the water. When she raised back up, she winced as her fingers caught in the tangles he had created. "I hope you have a comb, or it's going to take me a few hours to get rid of these tangles."

"Fresh out. But I'll be glad to comb it myself, when I get my hands on one."

The image of Joshua combing her hair set her heart racing and she remembered her lack of resistance to him just moments before. Shaking her head, she glanced at him warily. "No, thanks. I think I've had about all the help from you I can stand in one day."

He cupped her chin lightly. "Don't be so sure about that, pretty lady, or I'll take it as a challenge." He brushed his lips against hers quickly. "I don't know about you, but I used up just about all my reserves of self-control with you when we stopped kissing about five minutes ago. There's no denying the fire between us. You've knocked me off my feet.'' He shook his head at her protest and continued, "But now is not the time to discuss it. And you don't have to worry. I won't push you as long as you let me see you.'' Releasing her chin, he handed her an inner tube and grinned. "I found your inner tube. Now, get on down the river and earn your keep as a chaperone.''

Cassie stared at him blankly for a moment until she watched him push off into the rapids. She snatched her T-shirt from the side of the river, then lifted her body into her own tube and paddled after him fuming. Of all the nerve. What made him think he could dictate her actions. She felt totally confused. Perhaps, Cassie thought darkly, that was what he intended. In the last ten minutes, she'd practically made love to a man on a riverbank, gotten thrown in the water by the same man, been threatened by the man and instructed as to her behavior, yes, by the very same men.

Finding herself drifting toward some sharp rocks, Cassie decided she'd better focus her attention on the river instead of Joshua. She'd just have to deal with him later.

She finally made it to the designated meeting place and heard Kim call to her. "Where have you been, Cassie? You look like you got caught in a whirlpool.''

Cassie grimaced at the picture she knew she presented. Tangled hair, sunburned nose, no makeup. And to top it off, she felt whipped. The headache she'd noticed intermittently throughout the day settled into a dull pain, and her nose began to tingle uncomfortably. "Well, this little boy got away from his parents and . . .''

She stopped, too tired to discuss the frightening incident. "I'll tell you about it later. You wouldn't happen to have a comb, would you?" she asked hopefully.

Dragging the inner tube and her body from the river, she collapsed beside Kim, who was rummaging through a tote bag. Kim smiled and held up a comb. "Look what I found." She looked critically at Cassie's hair. "You'd better get started. It looks like it might take you a while."

Cassie glanced around warily and took the comb. "Thanks. You haven't seen Joshua around, have you?"

"He's with one of the kids. Apparently one of them got stung several times by a bee, and he's trying to keep everyone calm. I can get him for you if you want me to." Kim rose until Cassie clutched her arm.

"Oh, no, don't do that." When Kim looked at her quizzically, Cassie explained, "I mean, I wouldn't want to bother him if he's taking care of bee stings." She winced at the hair she was pulling from the comb. "Say, how are you and Fred getting home?"

"Some of the parents were nice enough to pick up the cars and bring them here. We'll be leaving in a few minutes."

The late afternoon air was beginning to cool and Cassie felt chilled. She sneezed. "Listen, Kim, I'm not feeling that great. Do you think Fred would mind dropping me off?"

A look of concern crossed Kim's face. "Of course not, but I'm sure Joshua would want to know. Let me get him."

"No . . ." Cassie watched Kim rush off to find Joshua. Great, she thought. Just when she thought she might get away without having to face Joshua again, her friend goes to get him for her. Cassie decided avoidance was the best route to take when dealing with Joshua. He upset her equilibrium. Every time he came near her, she felt like she was dry kindling and someone had just struck a match to her. The overwhelming physical attraction was enough to fight. But the clincher was that she had seen his caring side last night with his father. Right now, he comforted an upset teenager. When she considered writing off her attraction to Joshua as completely physical, his caring nature was her Waterloo.

She sneezed again and her head began to pound.

Joshua approached with a concerned expression. "What's wrong? Kim says you're not feeling well."

"Oh, I'm sure it's nothing critical. I've probably just gotten too much sun and water. I know you've got to stay here with the kids until all the parents show up. Kim said Fred wouldn't mind giving me a ride home."

He looked so torn that for a fleeting moment Cassie felt remorse for putting him in this position. Then, she sneezed again.

He sighed. "Listen, Cassie, I really want to see you home, but I can't leave these kids, and you look awful."

"Gee, thanks."

Ignoring her response, he looked at her carefully. "I'll stop by your house after I finish here."

"That's not necessary."

"Yes, it—"

Kim came up and put an arm around Cassie's shoulders. "Don't worry, Joshua, we'll get her home. By the way, have you found a location for your store?"

Joshua looked at Cassie and said, "Uh, yes."

In no mood to discuss Joshua's business plans, Cassie tensed and said politely, "Thank you for inviting me, Joshua. Good-bye."

"Wait." He put a hand on her arm.

Kim seemed oblivious to the undercurrents between them and continued her chatter. "That's great. Where'd you end up buying?"

Her headache, coupled with her weariness with the entire situation, depleted her usual supply of patience. She turned to leave with stiff movements as she answered Kim's question. "As a matter of fact, Joshua's buying my building . . . and kicking me out of it." She stalked off to Fred's car and didn't bother to look at Joshua and the grim expression on his face.

"Are you going to tell me about it or not?" Kim asked Cassie, turning around from the front seat.

"I really don't feel like talking about it, Kim. I've developed a monstrous headache within the last hour." Cassie couldn't tell if the headache was related to her sneezing or her jumbled feelings and thoughts about Joshua. He'd followed her back to the car, pinned her with that dark-brown gaze, and insisted that he would see her later. Momentarily, she'd wondered if he planned to jerk her out of the car and paddle her.

"Cassie, I'm not going to force you to talk about him, but I think you should know that Joshua doesn't mean anything personal by evicting you from your building. In fact, from what Fred tells me, he's so flipped out over you that—Ouch!" Kim glared at Fred who had nudged her sharply with his elbow. "Well, she ought to know, Fred."

"She ought to know what Joshua wants her to know.

Joshua didn't tell me his feelings about Cassie so you could go blabbing them to her.'' Fred pulled in front of Cassie's house.

Cassie could see the beginnings of an argument between her two friends and regretted that she was the cause of it. ''Listen, you two, don't fight over this. I'm sure Joshua's a fine person, but I don't see how a relationship between us is possible. He's taking away something that I've spent years working on, just when it's starting to pay for me. It's pretty hard for me to see past that right now.''

''No kidding,'' Fred said as he faced her, shaking his head. ''Cassie, you're only seeing this situation from your point of view. How do you think Joshua feels? He's got to do the very best that he can for his business because he has people depending on him—his partner, his employees. On the other hand, I'm sure he hates knowing that doing his best for his business means you could get hurt.''

Cassie considered Fred's words for a minute. She had been pretty self-centered in her perception of this situation. Perhaps it's been just as difficult for Joshua, she thought. Still, Joshua wasn't responsible for her shop, she was. Someone had to look out for Discriminating Pleasures.

She sighed. ''Fred, you've got a point, but I've got to watch out for my business, just as Joshua has to do his best for his business.'' Cassie sneezed and smiled weakly. ''Excuse me. Thanks for the ride and the advice.'' She opened the car door, waved to her friends, and walked to her house.

That evening, Cassie turned on her answering machine, ate some soup, and crawled into bed. She slept deeply, but when her alarm went off at seven the next morning, she was amazed at how tired she felt. Her throat was scratchy, her head pounded, and she couldn't breathe through her nose. She couldn't be sick, she thought. She hadn't been sick since college.

To be on the safe side, she took her temperature. One hundred and two degrees. Oh, hell. Just what she needed on a Monday morning. She dialed Maggie's number and breathed a sigh of relief when the older woman agreed to cover the store for her. Downing a couple of cold capsules with a glass of orange juice, she returned to bed.

She drifted in and out of sleep throughout the day, waking only to drink some water and go to the bathroom. She awoke to a pounding noise and was surprised to note that it was evening already. The pounding noise sounded again and Cassie wondered if it was inside her head or at the door. Lying very still, Cassie listened once again and heard a loud voice coupled with the knocking at the door.

Dragging on her robe, she stood unsteadily and walked to the door, noting that neither her throat nor her chills had improved. She swallowed and winced. "Who is it?"

"Cassie, open this door, or I swear I'll break it down."

Joshua. *Isn't that just like a man?* Cassie wondered what had happened to the more civilized approach of using the telephone. Unlocking the door, she pulled it open and stared at him. "I'm probably contagious, so you'd better go away." She started to close the door, but Joshua moved too quickly. Of course, her great-grandmother could have beat her at the speed at which she was moving.

Joshua stared in horror at Cassie. His gaze took in the red nose, dark circles under her droopy eyes, and a face flushed with fever. "Where have you been? I called you until eleven o'clock last night and several times today, and kept on getting your damned answering machine. At first, I thought you were still mad at me from yesterday. Then, I began to worry and I called the shop. Maggie told me you were sick so I came over when I finished having dinner with a client."

Cassie folded her arms around her and shivered. "You really didn't need to go to all that trouble, Joshua. I've just got a little cold."

Narrowing his eyes, he stepped closer and placed a hand on her forehead. "You're burning up. Have you taken your temperature or seen a doctor?"

Her head felt light, her knees weakened and she smiled as she tried to determine if her cold or Joshua was responsible for her maladies. He seemed to be talking so fast, moving so fast. She heard him repeat the question. Everything was spinning, and she murmured, "One hundred and two this morning . . ."

Then her knees buckled and she sank to the floor.

FIVE

Finding herself on the sofa with a blanket placed snugly around her, Cassie heard Joshua talking on her phone.

"I know this is above and beyond the call of duty, Clay, but I really appreciate it. I'll see you in about fifteen minutes." He replaced the receiver and walked back into the living room.

She shook off her mental fuzziness and eyed him warily. "Who's Clay, and where is he going to be in fifteen minutes?"

"Clay Jennings is a doctor friend of mine from high school and college, and he's coming here in fifteen minutes." When she started to protest, he continued with confidence, "Or I can take you to the emergency room."

"Emergency room! Joshua, have you lost your mind? You don't go to the emergency room for a cold. You're overreacting. You should call your friend back and I'll go see a doctor tomorrow. I just need a good night's sleep.''

He brought her a glass of water and held it to her lips. ''Pretty lady, you passed out on the floor less than five minutes ago, you've got a raging fever, and there's no way on God's green earth I'm going to leave you in this condition.'' Pushing her hair back from her heated forehead, he gazed at her tenderly. ''So, just relax and let Clay and me take care of you.

''What else can I get for you?'' He frowned as he studied her flushed cheeks and over-bright eyes. ''Do you want something else to drink? Where's your thermometer?''

The sight of Joshua fussing over her irritated her and warmed her heart at the same time. ''I'm fine. I don't need anything.'' She yawned and sank back into the sofa. ''And you're being very nice.''

His boyish smile charmed her woman's soul. ''What are friends for, Cassie?'' Clasping her hand in both of his, he continued deliberately, ''And I intend for us to be the very best of friends.''

''Friends?'' Cassie murmured the suggestion and turned the thought over in her head. Yes, he would be a great friend . . . if he weren't so damn sexy.

Joshua watched the varying emotions cross over her face—the furrowed brow showed her deep thoughtfulness, the softening in her eyes revealed compassion. The flame that briefly lit her eyes suggested she was remembering their passion on the side of the river. Gently, he entreated her, ''I want to be your friend. I want to be your lover, too.'' Although he felt her tense, he continued, ''It's too late to deny it. I've felt your heat and your touch. I've seen the passion in your eyes and tasted it on your lips. And I want all of you." He smiled at the shiver that ran through her at his words. "But most of all, I want to be your friend. Let's just take it slow, I'll do my best never to hurt you. Can you accept that?"

Although she longed to hide from her intense attraction, she had to admire his honesty. He wasn't pulling any punches, and he risked a great deal by speaking his mind. She saw a hint of vulnerability in his eyes, and a part of her melted at the sight of it. Cassie realized she wasn't being very gracious about him coming to her aid. She felt so tired. Perhaps she could let her guard down for just one night. How comforting it felt to let someone else be responsible for a little while.

Then, she thought of the masterful seducer he had been at the river and raised a skeptical eyebrow. "Slow?"

Laughing, he raised his hands in a helpless gesture. "I'll do my best, but you've got to remember that I find you an irresistible temptation."

"Then I'll just have to do my best to make myself more resistable." Although why any man would find her irresistible right now was beyond her. She was sure she looked a mess. Cassie sighed and closed her eyes until she felt the thermometer pressed to her lips.

"I found it on the counter." The door bell rang and Joshua brushed a tender kiss across her forehead as he popped the thermometer the rest of the way into her mouth. "That must be Clay. We'll get you fixed up."

After Joshua introduced her to Clay, the good doctor proceeded to poke, prod, and question her. She gagged and glared at him when he dabbed her swollen throat with a cotton swab.

"It looks like a nasty case of strep throat, but I'll know for sure after I drop this off at the lab. She definitely needed medical attention."

Joshua gave her a knowing smile, and she rolled her eyes in response.

"I'll call the antibiotic prescription into the all-night pharmacy, so you can pick it up, Josh." Clay continued to speak as if she weren't there. And if Cassie had felt just a tiny bit better, she would have protested. But she felt rotten and it hurt to talk, so she kept her mouth shut. "She needs to stay in bed for the next day or two."

Correctly interpreting Cassie's audible groan, Joshua squeezed her shoulder and reassured her. "Don't worry. I'll call Maggie. You just rest."

By this point, she was so sleepy that she obeyed. She vaguely remembered Joshua giving her some medication, but she had no recollection of crawling into bed when she woke the next morning. The thought of Joshua removing her robe and placing her in her bed added heat to her already feverish body. A woman couldn't ask for a more caring friend than Joshua had been last night, and Cassie felt moved by his consideration.

The phone rang loudly beside her ear, and she answered it quickly.

"Hello."

"Cassie, this is Maggie. Joshua called me last night, and I just wanted to check and see how you're doing. I've been worried about you."

"I'll be fine by tomorrow. I feel better already. It's amazing what antibiotics can do. I hope you don't mind working two full days in a row. What time is it, anyway?''

"Ten o'clock. And don't you dare worry about me working by myself at the store. I get to play boss with you gone. Besides that, you've got enough to worry about with finding us another location for the store. That Mr. Blomburg was here this morning when I got in. He took me by surprise. He wanted to know when we're planning on moving. When I said I didn't know, he told me not to worry about it and that Joshua was real persuasive and he always seemed to find a way to get what they needed.''

Cassie sat straight up in bed. Why that weasel! Going behind her back when she was sick, pretending to be her friend. She asked curtly, "What else did he say?''

"Oh, my,'' Maggie said. "I just assumed with Mr. Daniels taking care of you when you were sick that y'all had gotten this all talked out. I'm sorry I opened my big mouth.''

"Maggie, tell me what else he said.''

"Well,'' the older woman paused. "I didn't catch it all, but he muttered something about getting their lawyer to check to see if there were any loopholes in the lease. And then he said Joshua wanted to make some renovations and be ready for business in three months.''

"Well, Mr. Daniels is just going to have to learn that he can't have everything when he wants it and how he wants it. If Mr. Blomburg calls back, you tell him I'm not budging from that building until the last minute. If he thinks he can force me out before, then he can call *my* lawyer.''

"Oh, my.'' The dismay was evident in Maggie's

voice. "What do you want me to tell Joshua if he calls?"

"You just let me handle Mr. Daniels," Cassie replied hotly. "I may be a little weak from this sore throat, but I can handle his kind any day. Thanks for calling, Maggie."

After she hung up the phone, Cassie could scarcely contain herself, so she threw off her covers and stomped into the kitchen. On the counter beside her medicine, she saw a note from Joshua. He reminded her to take her medicine and get plenty of rest. She snorted when she read the part about how concerned he was about her and that he would check on her periodically throughout the day.

Well, if he thought she'd welcome him with open, grateful arms, he could just forget it. Forget friendship. The only thing Joshua Daniels was getting from her was a piece of her mind.

Cassie prepared some toast and ate it along with some juice. As she washed the few dishes at the sink, she heard a sound at the door. She saw the knob turn and wondered who it could be. Only Kim and her next-door neighbor had a key.

The door opened and Joshua walked in with a bouquet of flowers. The flowers distracted her momentarily. Then, she remembered his deception.

Cassie crossed her arms defensively over her chest. "What are you doing here?"

His grin lit up his entire face. "Well, I've come to see how my favorite lady is doing."

Famous last words, Cassie thought. It distressed her that she noticed he looked and smelled good enough to eat, but she didn't allow it to deter her from her purpose. When he reached to touch her, she ducked and moved away.

"And just why is it that your favorite lady is the last to know that you've asked your lawyers to check for loopholes in my lease so you can get me out of your building?" She studied his face intently, almost hoping he'd have an explanation, until she saw the shadow cross his face.

"I haven't consulted my lawyers about looking for loopholes, although I must admit I'm going to be pretty desperate if I'm not moved in by August." His eyebrows furrowed. "Where did you hear this?"

"Maggie called this morning with a message from your beloved partner requesting that I speed up my exit from your property."

"You're kidding," Joshua looked incredulous.

"Oh, don't give me that innocent look." Cassie glared at him accusingly. "I almost bought that caring act you played out last night." She held up a hand when he tried to interrupt her. "What a fool I've been. Mr. Blomburg told Maggie all about how you use your persuasive abilities to get what you want. If you think getting me into your bed is going to get you into my building any sooner, then you can just forget it. You may end up with that property, but I'll make it darned difficult for you to get anything done until I get out."

Joshua's face was tight with anger when he responded. "You have got to be the most suspicious female I've ever met in my life." He shoved the flowers into her hands. "I came here last night because, for some strange reason, I care about you." He gave a sarcastic half-smile. "I was trying to be considerate. But if this is the result of being considerate, perhaps I'd better try a colder, more business-like approach. I don't know what my partner said, but I thought you knew me well enough to know that I wouldn't use deception to further my business. Enjoy the flowers, Cassie." He tossed the key onto her counter and said, "Here's your key. I doubt I'll need it anymore."

Cassie watched in open-mouthed stupefaction as he strode out her door.

In the days that followed, Cassie wavered back and forth in her feelings about Joshua Daniels. It had all sounded pretty damning. But he had oozed integrity when she had accused him. A sinking sensation settled in her stomach. The more she thought about it, the more it seemed that his business partner may have been expressing his admiration of Joshua's social abilities. And when she added her additional pangs of missing Joshua, it all added up to a big mess.

Cassie had spent the better part of the week in the frustrating exercise of finding another location for her shop, so she was relieved at the prospect of temporarily escaping her problems at her family reunion that weekend.

She drove to her hometown on Saturday night, joined in the picnic on Sunday, and drove back on the same day. She found that, although she enjoyed seeing her brothers and nieces, the uncertain future of her shop and her feelings about Joshua hung over her like a dark cloud. Her father and mother had commented on her preoccupation, and she strongly suspected that her brother Ben's unexpected plan to pay her a visit in the next few days was due to her family's concern.

After a restless night, Cassie firmly resolved to get

her life in order. If she had to move out of the downtown area, then that's what she'd do. But she was determined to pull herself out of the funk she seemed to be in. She frowned as she saw police cars parked in front of her shop. Two uniformed men walked through the door of the neighboring dress shop, while speaking with the distressed owner.

Cassie ran quickly to the owner's side. "What's going on, Mrs. Freeman? Have you been robbed? Is someone hurt?"

The elderly woman sobbed and shook her head. "No, it's much worse. Just look at what they've done to my shop, Cassie."

A gasp escaped her lips as she perused her neighbor's dress shop. Obscenities were written in black paint on the wall. Clothes were strewn all over the place, ripped apart, ruined and stained by the black paint. The cash register had been thrown on the floor upside down. Apparently, the perpetrators had been frustrated at finding it empty because it was broken into several pieces.

"Vandals," Cassie whispered.

"That's right," a gritty male voice said. "This is the third downtown store hit in as many weeks." The middle-aged policeman shook his head and removed the hat from his balding head. "And this is the worst yet. We'll put out extra night patrols."

"Do you have any idea who did this?" Cassie asked.

"None. It looks like something a group of teenagers would do. We'll be checking out the local schools." He turned to Mrs. Freeman with a sympathetic expression on his face. "I'll be in touch when we hear something. Sorry your Monday had to start out this way. If you have any problems with your insurance agency, you have them call me, ya hear?"

Mrs. Freeman's voice trembled, "Thank you, officer." She turned to Cassie. "Oh, Cassie, what in the world am I going to do? Many of these dresses came from France, and can't be reordered due to the change in seasons. The policeman told me I was lucky. At least I have insurance. The other business owners didn't have adequate coverage."

Cassie murmured her sympathy and gave the older woman a gentle hug. She offered her the use of her phone, since Mrs. Freeman's had been torn from the wall.

When Maggie came in, Cassie sent her to Mrs. Freeman's to help out until lunchtime. Cassie called her realtor and scheduled appointments for viewing locations out of the downtown area, accepting the fact that she was going to have to move soon, so she'd better do something about it.

Just as she set her mind to making plans for a clearance sale, Cassie watched Joshua walk through the door. And at the same time she felt her heart surge into her throat. "Joshua."

His gaze fell over her with something close to panic in his eyes. "Cassie, are you okay? I just heard the news about the vandals on the radio. But the reporter only mentioned the street name, without the name of the shop. I was afraid something had happened to . . ."

Cassie felt her heart sink at his statement. He'd only been worried about his precious building. He wasn't concerned about her. "As you can see, your property is perfectly safe. No unsightly black paint to mar the walls or anything else vandals tend to leave in their wake.''

Confusion crossed his strong face. "My property?" Then, recognition dawned and frustration reigned. "To hell with the building. I was afraid something might have happened to you. The news was sketchy . . . Oh, forget it. I'm glad you're safe.'' He thrust his fingers through his hair in exasperation and turned to leave.

Cassie hesitated only a second. Perhaps, he did care about her. She'd never seen Joshua so flustered. "Wait!''

Stopping in his tracks, he turned and looked at her expectantly.

"Uh, it was the dress shop next door that got vandalized.'' She paused. "Nobody was hurt.'' *Oh, God, what else should she say?*

He nodded but said nothing.

He wasn't going to make this easy for her. Perhaps she didn't deserve to have it easy after she'd misread him. Taking a deep breath, she said, "It was nice of you to be concerned about me.''

He watched but still said nothing.

Desperate to keep him from leaving, Cassie blurted out, "It was nice of you to be concerned about me today . . . and last week when I was sick.''

He relaxed his stance and shoved his hands into his pockets. The position was typically male, but she noticed that his face seemed less wary, even though he still hadn't spoken.

With one last deep breath, Cassie said, "I acted like a jerk last week, and I'm sorry.''

His whole demeanor changed and he strolled over to where she stood next to the counter. His face was serious, but a determined glint sparked in his eyes. "How sorry?"

Cassie swallowed. "Very sorry."

He stepped close enough to her that his breath whispered against her face, and she felt her blood surge through her veins at his nearness. His gaze raked over her face, and Cassie would have sworn that she detected a longing in his brown eyes that matched her own.

For a long moment, he stared intently at her lips, and Cassie held her breath. It seemed an eternity had passed since either had spoken. *Was he going to kiss her?* God, she hoped so.

But he didn't. Backing away from her, he shrugged. "No problem."

And then, he walked out the door leaving Cassie staring after him open-mouthed once again.

No problem! She poured her guts out to the man, humbly offered him an apology, after which he had looked at her like he was going to eat her on the spot and then he said, "No problem."

Cassie shook her head. She would never understand men. Even having two brothers had never prepared her for Joshua.

As he pulled his Trans Am out of the no-parking zone, Joshua wondered if he should have been so flip with Cassie's apology. He'd been about a half inch away from kissing her senseless before he'd pulled back. Although he hated seeing her so uncomfortable, she'd hurt him with her accusations. *Face it, Daniels, the woman's lack of trust stings your ego*. He'd spent the last week walking around with such a lost expression it was a wonder someone hadn't thrown him in the dog pound.

Deciding he'd give her a few days to squirm like he had, Joshua flipped on the radio and hummed along for the first time in a week.

Cassie smiled affectionately at the handsome man sprawled on her sofa. Ben was regaling her with stories of his latest escape from the clutches of matrimony.

"Ben, you bring it on yourself. Women take one look at you with your curly hair and soulful eyes, and decide they need to take you home and take care of you. They have no idea that there's a wolf behind that boyish face of yours."

With a wounded expression, Ben sat up straight. "Well, I see I'll get no sympathy from you. Even my very own sister is against me."

She laughed and punched him playfully. "Come on, big brother, if I can't give you sympathy, I can at least get you to food. I believe you requested Joe's Bar and Grill. Let's go before I change my mind and fix you a hot dog."

Ben stood quickly and made a face. "I get enough of them on the road." He offered his arm. "My chariot awaits."

On the way to the restaurant, Cassie filled Ben in on her difficulty in finding another location for her shop. He sympathized with her problems and encouraged her to keep looking.

As they walked through the restaurant door, he wrapped his arm around her consolingly. "Cass, if there's anyone who can work this out, I know you can. You need to remember how you built that business up from the bottom. You're just feeling a little discouraged. Is this why you were acting so out of sorts this weekend?''

"Mostly." She reached up to peck him on the cheek. "But thanks for the vote of confidence. I can use it right now."

When the hostess directed them to their table, Cassie failed to notice the trio of men seated on the other side of the room.

But, Joshua, Fred, and Jack noticed her. Fred cocked his head at the table where Cassie and Ben sat. "Hey, who's the new guy with Cassie? Josh, I thought you and she were . . ." Fred's voice trailed off when he looked at Joshua's stunned gaze.

Joshua barely heard Fred; he was too busy watching Cassie. As the couple strolled through the door, he'd done a doubletake when he saw the guy give her an affectionate squeeze. His jaw had almost hit the floor when he watched Cassie kiss the stranger on the cheek. A sick feeling tore through his gut at the sight of their heads bowed close in conversation. He'd trade the title to his car, if someone would give him the secret to having Cassie treat him with the easy affection she was treating the guy she'd walked in with.

Jack interrupted his thoughts. "He looks familiar. I don't know what it is, but there's something about him."

Fred studied the tall, blond man. "Do you think he's from around here?" He frowned. "Wait a minute. Isn't she from Holly Beach? Maybe he's from her hometown."

"Whoever he is," said Fred, "they look pretty cozy."

Joshua grimly agreed.

* * *

"So, how's your love life, little sister?"

Cassie grimaced. "Not nearly as exciting as yours."

Ben sighed and turned serious. "Speaking of your love life, I saw Billy Joe Hart at a bar in Holly Beach last night. When he asked about you, I told him I was paying you a visit. I even told him I'd finagled you into taking me out for dinner here tonight." He rubbed his jaw thoughtfully and continued. "You know, I'd always thought Billy Joe was a real jerk for what he did to you, but after seeing him last night, I'm beginning to think he did you a favor. He hasn't even turned thirty and he's already been through two wives."

After taking a long swallow of beer, he studied Cassie. "You're not still hung up on him after all this time, are you?"

Cassie's eyes widened in surprise. "Hung up on Billy Joe? Are you kidding?"

She watched Ben shake his head in response. "Oh, Ben, I think I got over Billy Joe within a week of when he eloped." Looking away from his inquiring gaze, she exhaled deeply. "The humiliation of having the whole town know about my personal affairs, dealing with Mom and Dad's embarrassment, that's what really bothered me. It seemed that everywhere I turned someone was whispering about Billy Joe and the girl he got pregnant—and poor Cassie. I couldn't stand it. Things really changed for the better when I moved here where no one knew about my engagement."

"Maybe so, but when are you gonna get back on the horse and start dating again." Ben watched Cassie begin to protest and shook his head. "And I don't mean these friends you go out with occasionally. I mean a real rip-your-guts-out relationship." He paused momentarily, then added, "Complete with sex."

"Sex!"

"Yeah, sex." Ben nodded patiently. "It's when a man and a woman—"

"I know what sex is," Cassie interrupted his explanation. "I just never expected to get this kind of advice from my older brother, considering how you used to put my dates through the third degree."

Ben shrugged. "I'm not advising you to be fast and loose. But, you're all tense and jumpy, Cassie. For Pete's sake, you're a grown woman. You need a man in your life. There must be somebody you're attracted to."

Embarrassed by her brother's remarks, Cassie shot back, "If that isn't like a man. I'm a tense, jumpy, grown woman, therefore I need a man. Really, Ben."

Ben leaned back in his chair, and noticed the color in her cheeks. "You're protesting too much, and you still haven't answered my question. Is there anybody you're attracted to?"

This was just like Ben—persistent, intuitive, obnoxious. She should have known he was going to grill her when he told her he planned to visit her. And when Ben put on his big-brother hat, there was no way he was going to take it off until he was satisfied his baby sister was doing fine.

"You know you're being obnoxious, don't you?"

With a crafty grin, he nodded, "Some things never change. Spill the beans, Cass."

Cassie rolled her eyes and admitted defeat. "As a matter-of-fact, I've met someone who is very attractive."

Ben waited expectantly.

"But there is a problem," Cassie said, "actually there's more than one problem. But, the biggest problem is that the man to whom I'm attracted is . . ."

Revealing his impatience, Ben said, "Is what? Is married, is in prison, is a priest?"

Cassie giggled in response. "No, although he is a minister's son. He's buying my building. He could very well be responsible for causing me to lose my business."

"Aw, come on, Cassie. You don't really believe that, do you?" The waiter brought their meal and Ben waited until he left. Sighing heavily, Ben spoke slowly, as if he was speaking to a child, "Cass, someone is going to buy your building. If it wasn't this guy— what's this guy's name?"

"Joshua."

"Right," he nodded. "If Joshua doesn't buy it, then someone else will. You're gonna be out of that building no matter who buys it. If you really want to blame someone, I guess you could blame your landlord. But, I think your energy would be better spent finding yourself a new location for your shop." Picking up his steak sandwich, he glanced at her doubtfully. "I'm surprised at you. Are you sure you're not using this as a smoke-screen because you're really scared?"

Cassie didn't respond immediately. Picking up her sandwich, she mulled over her brother's reasoning in her mind. Was she really that much of a coward? Joshua made her feel tingly, happy, aroused, and . . . scared. She'd have to think that over some more.

Ben interrupted her thoughts. "You didn't answer my question."

"I'm not going to." She glanced at him warningly. "Don't push, Ben. I'll think about it." Changing the subject, she noticed that Ben had finished his entire sandwich. "What did you do? Inhale your meal? I could have sworn the waiter just set this stuff on the table."

He grinned sheepishly and shrugged. "What can I say? I'm a growing boy." Gazing across the room, he raised his hand in response to someone at the bar. "Hey, there's a guy I went to college with. Do you mind if I go talk to him? Geez, I haven't seen him in about ten years."

Waving him off, Cassie said, "Go ahead, I'll be fine."

Cassie stared down at the remainder of her sandwich with intense interest, while her thoughts again returned to Joshua. She was so consumed with them that she failed to notice the man approaching her table until he spoke to her.

"Hi, Cassie. I've been trying to get in touch with you. I would've tried to see you on Sunday if I'd known you were in Holly Beach." Billy Joe smiled lazily at her astonished face. "Looks like I had to follow you here to get your attention."

Barely stifling a groan, Cassie wondered what perverse demon was getting his jollies at her expense today. She watched in abject horror as Billy Joe pulled a chair next to hers and took her hand. The smell of liquor on his breath coupled with his slurred speech and bloodshot eyes led her to believe that he'd been using a bottle to bolster his courage.

Although she tugged mightily to retrieve her hand from his, he held tight. Cassie sighed in frustration and turned her head in a vain search for Ben. Where was her brother when she needed him?

"Now that I've got your attention, I think I'll keep it, along with you." He leaned forward, his intent evident in the way he stared at her mouth.

SIX

Taking a long swallow of beer, Joshua shook his head at the sight he beheld. How many men did the woman have, anyway? At this rate, he'd have to take a number to see her. He smiled grimly to himself, knowing he'd never do that for a woman. His pride wouldn't allow it, although he found himself wishing he hadn't been so flip with her apology yesterday.

This second man was tall and blonde, too. She must have a thing for blondes. He momentarily mourned his dark hair, then cursed himself for even caring. He'd never had a problem attracting women before.

After a futile attempt to look away from her, Joshua studied Cassie and the man. He was relieved that Fred and Jack had joined a dart game so he wouldn't have to pretend disinterest. At least she wasn't smiling. As a matter-of-fact, he could swear she was trying to remove her hand from his. He watched the distress on her features as the guy leaned toward her.

Joshua took another swallow of beer and wondered if he should go over to her table, just in case she was in trouble.

Then, he watched her take care of the problem herself. Cassie shook her honey-blonde curls and pushed the guy hard, onto the floor.

Cassie winced at the sight of Billy Joe sprawling on the floor. She hated scenes with a passion and with Billy Joe drunk and angry at her it appeared that this one was going to be a doozy.

"Problems?" Cassie whipped around at the sound of Joshua's low voice. A tingle ran down her spine when she met the intent gaze that belied his casual posture. At that moment, he seemed so strong and steady that she briefly considered throwing herself into his arms and begging him to take her away from here. But Billy Joe was rousing himself from the floor with a mean scowl on his face.

"Just a misunderstanding," she murmured in response to his question as she clasped and unclasped her hands.

The two men sized each other up in their own style; Billy Joe with his chest puffed out and his rounded chin tilted at an arrogant angle. Cassie felt Joshua's body grow taut, but noticed that the only visible change in his demeanor was his shuttered facial expression and narrowed eyes.

With an evil glint in his eyes, Billy Joe drawled, "Is this one of your latest boyfriends, Cassie? Have you told him about the men in your past?" He paused, then taunted. "Have you told him that you were once engaged to me?"

Joshua watched Cassie's face flush with color as she

answered him in a low voice, "That was a long time ago. It's all over now."

Joshua didn't like this guy one bit. Although he didn't usually resort to physical violence, he found the idea of ridding this guy of his teeth immensely appealing. The man was drunk, mean, and harassing the woman that he wanted for his own. The primitive instinct to protect drove Joshua to move closer to her side.

Billy Joe scoffed. "You're not saying you don't want me anymore? Why don't you tell this preppie boy to go on back to his table so we can have some privacy?"

Cassie swallowed down the lump of dread in her throat. Billy Joe was going to expose her deepest vulnerability to Joshua. She could tell by the ugly sneer on his face that he was bent on revenge, if she didn't give into him. What would Joshua think of her when he found out? Although she was reluctant to admit it, she cared a great deal about Joshua Daniels' opinion of her.

She tried logic. "Billy Joe, there's nothing between us anymore. We're different people now, with different lives. We're grown up."

Detesting Billy Joe for bringing that desperate tone to her voice, Joshua stepped in front of Cassie. "You're making Cassie nervous and she's not interested. So, why don't you move on to someone else?" Joshua shrugged. "There's plenty of action here."

But Billy Joe wasn't buying. Like a dog with a bone, he refused to let go. Lunging forward, he stood face to face with Joshua. "Why don't you stay out of it, and go get your own action?" His eyes shifted from Cassie to Joshua, somehow sensing the thread of emotion between the two of them. When Joshua didn't move away, he took his best shot. "Hey, I don't know what's going on between you two, but Cassie was mine before she even knew you. Do you get my drift? I made it with her in the backseat—"

Joshua broke off Billy Joe's revelation with an abrupt crack from his fist, which sent the insulting man sprawling to the floor for the second time that evening.

"Oh, my God," whispered Cassie taking in the sight of Billy Joe on the floor with a dazed expression on his face. People curiously crowded around them, stepping in front of her, and she heard their voices. But it all seemed surreal to her. This couldn't be happening. She hadn't experienced anything this mortifying since her cancelled wedding. And revulsion filled her at the thought of what Billy Joe had said about her before Joshua punched him.

Pushing through the eager crowd, Joshua felt his heart clench at the sight of Cassie's pinched, pale face and cursed himself for not taking Billy Joe out before he uttered his crude words. He put his hands gently on her shoulders until she lifted her distressed eyes to his, and he felt her misery as if it were his own.

"Oh, Cassie," he said as he wrapped his arms around her and folded her to him. Her body trembled slightly. Then, she relaxed against him and lay her head on his chest. Joshua's heart pounded with masculine pride with the realization that Cassie had trustingly enfolded herself in his protective arms.

"Hey, who the hell knocked out Billy Joe?"

Joshua's head whipped around at the blonde man loudly asking the question. He noticed this was the man that Cassie had arrived with tonight. Fine time for this guy to show up. Reluctantly, he pulled away from Cassie, wondering if he was going to have to use his normally peaceful fist again this evening.

He turned to face the man and calmly said, "I did."

Totally surprising Joshua, the man's face broke into a wide grin. "Well, it's about time. Let me shake your hand."

Doubtfully, Joshua extended his hand to the man. "Hey, I'm Ben Warner, Cassie's brother, and I've been waiting for years to punch this guy out, but Cassie made me swear to leave him alone."

Cassie's brother? Relief flowed through Joshua as realization dawned. That's why Cassie had appeared so familiar with him. Noting the resemblance in Ben's light hair and blue-green eyes, Joshua grinned.

"Pleased to meet you. I'm Joshua Daniels."

A light of recognition and something Joshua couldn't identify flashed through Ben's eyes. "Joshua, huh?" He gestured to the still-reclining figure of Billy Joe. "We wouldn't want to leave this kind of mess on the floor. How about if I pack Billy up and let him sleep off his excesses at that hotel down the street?"

Joshua nodded his agreement. "Sounds good to me. Do you want some help?"

"Nah, I think I might enjoy doing it myself." Ben grinned, then looked around the room. "Say, where's Cassie?"

Reeling around to look at the empty spot where Cassie had been, Joshua swore under his breath and ran his fingers through his hair in exasperation. "I'll go after her. Did she drive?"

"No." Ben looked worried. "What did Billy Joe say, anyway?"

"Let me put it this way, he's lucky it only took one punch to put him out of commission." Joshua thumped Ben on the back. "Look, if I don't want Cassie walking around out there by herself in the dark, then I'd better get going. I'll see you later."

Joshua brushed through the crowd and hurried out the door. When he reached the street, he squinted his eyes, searching in both directions for a sign of Cassie. Then he took off at a dead run.

Escape. That was all Cassie had been able to think about when the people had begun to crowd around her and Joshua. She needed to catch her breath. The amused curiosity on their faces reminded her of that time so long ago when Billy Joe had eloped, just one day before their wedding, with the girl he'd gotten pregnant.

She'd worked so hard to leave that particular humiliation behind in Holly Beach, so that it wouldn't affect her here. She'd told no one about her broken engagement, not even Kim. Amazing how everything could change in a moment's time. Cringing, Cassie wondered if Billy Joe was spreading his torrid little version of their tale even at this moment. Don't even think about it, she admonished herself.

Cassie wondered if she could stand the humiliation again and laughed hysterically. Perhaps, she could move to Alaska this time. After all, she had no man in her life. Her store was going to fold. That's it, Alaska. She felt giddy at the thought. She could become an ice fisherman and live out her days alone in an igloo.

Hearing the rhythmic thud of footsteps on the pavement behind her, Cassie tensed as she realized her foolishness at walking in this section of town at night. Poised for flight, she spotted a hotel up ahead and began to walk swiftly toward it.

When she felt a hand on her shoulder, she froze with terror and a scream locked in her throat. The man's exaggerated breath whooshed against the back of her head. As she was pulled abruptly against a hard male body, Cassie struggled until she recognized his voice.

"Cassie," Joshua demanded as he caught his breath, "what do you think you're doing walking around this part of town alone at night? Are you crazy?"

Heaving a sigh of relief, Cassie braced herself against him and shook her head. "I had to get out of there. There were too many people around."

His penetrating gaze held a mixture of concern and irritation, and she pushed away from him, unable to bear his scrutiny. She'd been stripped to the bone by Billy Joe's statements and she felt raw and exposed. "He was drunk . . . and getting cruder by the minute." She clasped her hands together to relieve their trembling and helplessly glanced back at Joshua. "I just couldn't stay."

Joshua drew her back to him with a gentle touch to her arm and tilted her chin with a calloused finger. When he gazed into her eyes, she could have sworn he saw her soul. An expression of disbelief, then compassion, crossed over his face and he swept her into his arms.

"Ah, Cassie, you don't really think anybody who knows you would listen to that guy. Honey, he was such a jerk." His gentle rocking motion and husky, reassuring tone soothed and stirred her at the same time, and she laid her head against his strong chest. Unaccountably relieved that his opinion of her hadn't lessened with Billy Joe's words, she relaxed against him, enjoying the steady beat of his heart and his masculine scent.

His deep voice rumbled against her ear. "Though, I must confess that if you ever were engaged to him, I'm glad it fell through. It'd be pure hell to fall this hard for a married woman."

Wearing a gentle smile, he pulled slightly away to look into her face again. "I think this calls for a heavy dose of Rocky Road ice cream. Are you game?"

His gaze warmed her to her toes and she almost agreed, until she remembered Ben. "Oh, no," Cassie said with obvious disappointment, "Ben's staying with me. He's probably crazy with worry right now."

Joshua shook his head and touched the curve of her jaw with a light caress of his thumb. "Ben was taking care of Billy Joe and he's got the key to your apartment. I told him I was going after you." Involuntarily, Cassie turned her head to his touch, and watched his eyes heat at her action. "So, let's go to my place," he said.

Feeling her heart skip a beat as he drew her closer once again, Cassie said, "I don't want to impose on your mother."

He nuzzled against her hair. "I don't live with my mom. I've got a furnished place until I have more time to spend picking something out. I learned a long time ago that we're both a lot better off if I visit her instead of live with her." He put his mouth a breath away from hers and whispered, "What's the verdict?"

Mesmerized, she deliberated only a second, then whispered back, "Yes."

And he closed the minuscule distance between their lips with a teasing caress.

Cassie's feet were stretched out alongside Joshua's on his generic coffee table in his generic apartment. She missed his watchful gaze as she thoroughly licked the remains of her favorite ice cream from her lips. "Doesn't it bother you to live in such an impersonal place?"

He shrugged and turned his attention to her wavy hair, idly twirling a finger through a wayward curl. "I know I'm gonna be busy setting up this new location. I'll find something later."

Cassie shivered at the sensually intense light in his eyes. Caught in his gaze, her nerve endings hummed with electrical awareness. She knew she was vulnerable tonight and that she should leave, but she couldn't find the will. Too fascinated by the feelings he stirred within her, she merely waited, hoping.

But she didn't have to wait long.

Joshua took in the languid expression in her aqua eyes and felt his blood begin to flame. He was hot for her every time he was around her, but this was something else. When he watched her lick her lips, Joshua had wanted to stop her and do it himself. Studying her moist lips, he decided he might still do it.

He tangled the hair on either side of her head with his hands and gently tugged. "Come to me, Cassie." He watched her eyes darken as she moved closer. And he laid his questing lips upon her soft ones. He absorbed the whisper of her sigh and licked the corner of her lips.

Cassie looped her arms around his neck and stretched

her fingers into the thick hair that reached down to his nape. She smiled at the shiver that ran through him and opened her mouth in invitation. His large hands trailed down her neck to cup her breasts, flicking his thumbs across her sensitive nipples, burning her straight to her core. The unfamiliar sensations coursed through her and a faint alarm sounded in the back of her mind when he deepened the kiss and slowly pushed her beneath him on the sofa. But, like a forbidden dessert, Joshua was too delicious to resist. And she matched his ardor in the mating of their tongues.

She felt his hard arousal against her thigh, and instead of being frightened found that his wanting increased her own. She arched against him, needing to assuage the ache he had caused in her.

"Ah, Cassie," Joshua murmured hoarsely, "let's get rid of these clothes so I can show you how much I want you."

Cassie was too far gone to do anything but agree, until the telephone rang. Staring at each other, they both considered whether to ignore the untimely interruption or not. When the ringing continued, Joshua closed his eyes and groaned as he rose with obvious reluctance from the sofa and curtly answered the phone.

After he determined the identity of the caller, he said, "This had better be damn good, Blomburg."

Recalling the name of his business partner, Cassie sat up and smoothed her disheveled clothing. He turned his back to her, speaking in a low voice, and she considered leaving the room. On the heels of their passion, the reality of Joshua's business and his intent to evict her from his building put a bad taste in her mouth. She needed some space and decided to locate the bathroom.

Cassie could have kicked herself. What in the world was wrong with her? Her hormones must be shutting down all of her mental capabilities. Viewing herself in the mirror, she confronted her reflection and admitted her strong—no, make that very strong—attraction to Joshua. The flushed cheeks, swollen lips, and mussed hair told an undeniable story. But what to do about it?

Perhaps she should just give into her lust and get him out of her system. Still, there was this niggling doubt in the back of her mind that told her it wouldn't be that easy. He invaded her dreams, interrupted her normal thought patterns, and that was when he wasn't even in her presence.

And even though Joshua was pursuing her with a vengeance right now, Cassie believed that once he'd had enough of her he'd drop her like a hot potato. Joshua didn't strike her as the kind of man to whom personal commitment would come easily. Of course, the possibility existed that her fantasies of his lovemaking were better than the real thing. Cassie suspected that possibility was remote. Then she remembered his intention to take away her building and shook her head. She couldn't get involved with him with this mess hanging over them. It was just bad timing. After splashing her face with cool water and smoothing her hair, Cassie returned to the den to ask Joshua to take her home.

After she voiced her request, he stared at her with obvious frustration. "Why? You sure didn't say anything about going home ten minutes ago."

"I know," she answered defensively. "But the telephone call brought me to my senses." She held up her hand as he came toward her and opened his mouth in response. "I'm not denying that I'm attracted to you, Joshua. I'm only saying that this attraction is totally useless right now with you taking my building away from me."

She shrugged her shoulders helplessly. "I can't help it. I resent it and I resent you for doing it."

"But, Cassie, that's business. Can't you separate the two?" When he watched her shake her head, he threw up his arms in exasperation. "You know, men don't have this problem. We're perfectly capable of slitting each other's throat in business and going out for a beer afterward."

Cassie smiled at his logic. If she were a man, they wouldn't be experiencing this undeniable attraction. "That may be true, but, as you've discovered, I'm not a man. If it makes you feel better to blame your frustration on my gender, fine, but take me home."

When he saw her resolute expression, he gave a sigh of defeat. "Okay, just so you realize that you're only prolonging the inevitable. We're not finished."

Cassie felt the heat of his gaze clear down to her toes and knew he was right. She turned toward the door and realized she was only buying time.

The next day after work, Cassie kicked off her shoes, tossed her pocketbook onto an end table, and plopped down on her sofa with a loud groan. She lay in a prone position for about sixty seconds, then jerked herself upright. Although it had been less than twenty-four hours since she'd seen Joshua, it seemed like forever. Her sensitized body had kept her awake for hours, Ben grilled her this morning about her feelings for Joshua, and she'd spent the better part of the afternoon scouting out questionable locations for her shop.

She should be dead on her feet and ready for bed. But thoughts of Joshua lurked in the back of her mind all day, and she felt strangely edgy. Noting that the time was only eight o'clock, Cassie decided to go running. Surely, she reasoned, if she wore out her body completely, she'd be able to get a good night's sleep tonight. She was going to have to make a decision soon about what to do with Joshua. Even if she was able to control her mind, which wasn't likely, her body was not going to be persuaded to forget him. Joshua had awakened her, and she suspected that her desire for him matched his for her.

Just as she finished lacing her running shoes, her doorbell rang. Not feeling particularly sociable, she hoped she could get rid of whoever had come calling.

Cassie opened the door to Joshua dressed in running shorts, an old cut-off T-shirt, and worn tennis shoes. She mentally shook her head at how disgustingly sexy this man could look in such ragged clothing. His wide shoulders seemed to shrink her doorway. The taut chest and flat belly with the arrow of curly hair that disappeared into his shorts made her swallow hard to get past the lump in her throat.

Darn it! How was she supposed to eradicate his image from her mind when he presented such a spectacular picture to her in the flesh? And oh, how his flesh beckoned her to touch and explore. Joshua's sensuous brown eyes seemed to invite her pleasure.

Cassie shook her head and cleared her throat. "So, what brings you here?" she tried to say lightly and hoped he didn't notice the huskiness in her voice.

Joshua grinned and stared appreciatively at her exposed legs. "We must be telepathic. I remember you saying that you used to run in high school, so I thought we might take a little jog together."

She couldn't exactly say she wasn't planning to run, being dressed the way she was, but she still wasn't comfortable with the idea of being near him. "Well, I really wasn't—"

"Of course," he shrugged carelessly, "if you don't think you can keep up . . ." His voice trailed off.

Narrowing her eyes at his smug expression, Cassie couldn't resist such a macho challenge. And, she reasoned, what could possibly happen while they were running? "Oh, I think I might be able to keep up." Then, she said with exaggerated concern, "You won't go too far or too fast, will you?"

"I'll let you set the pace," Joshua said in a reassuring tone. "And when you get tired, we'll stop."

Tired, my fanny, thought Cassie. She smiled sweetly. "Let me get my key."

After following her street, they headed for the park, speaking little. For the first few miles, Cassie enjoyed the exercise and their quiet companionship. But when they started on their fifth mile, and Joshua was barely sweating, she developed a stitch in her side and began to wonder just how much running Joshua did on a regular basis. She had assumed, perhaps erroneously, that he wouldn't have time for running since he was so committed to his business. She slowed and grabbed her side, "I . . . have to . . . slow down," she said breathlessly. "Stitch."

Joshua slowed immediately and placed his hand at her waist. "Where is it? Right here?" She nodded as he pressed firmly. "If you press it for a minute or two, it should go away."

Cassie nodded and gulped in more air. Feeling his warm, strong hand on her waist wasn't doing her breathing one bit of good, and she gently nudged his hand away, replacing it with her own. "Thanks. I guess I'd forgotten that little trick."

He pointed to a bench, and folded her hand within his. "Let's rest for a minute."

She slumped down on the bench and closed her eyes as she tipped her head back. When she felt his gaze on her, she opened her eyes and said with a wry smile, "Okay, I give. How much do you usually run, Joshua?"

He grinned mischievously in return. "Well," he paused. "I haven't run any marathons . . . in at least six months."

"Marathons!" Cassie groaned. "I was certain you were too busy with your business to run much on a regular basis. And when you smugly suggested that I couldn't keep up with you, I figured I'd teach you a lesson or two." She smiled sheepishly. "Looks like I'm the one who got taught this time." Then, with a laugh, she said, " I guess there's always darts."

Joshua laughed at her competitive spirit. "Yeah, there's always darts. Besides, we've run close to five miles at a pretty fast clip. That's pretty good for a—"

"If you're going to say for a woman, I'll personally box your ears, Joshua Daniels," Cassie threatened.

Covering his ears protectively, Joshua replied, "Uh, no, I wasn't going to say that. I was going to say for someone who hasn't run in a long time."

"Sure," Cassie said with disbelief.

Their laughs faded, and they settled into a companionable silence. Cassie relaxed and enjoyed the evening sounds of the crickets and a distant train. She revelled in the sensation of the cool evening air on her skin.

"So, when are you going to tell me about Billy Joe?"

Every muscle in her body tensed at his question. He'd seemed so sensitive to her needs last night by avoiding a discussion of the scene Billy Joe had made. And she had been relieved she didn't have to explain.

"Perhaps some other time," she said and thought, like when I'm eighty years old and can laugh about it all. "This has been a great run." Cassie stood with a forced smile pasted on her face. "But if we don't get moving, I'm gonna have to hail a cab." She waited, hoping that he wouldn't press the issue.

She felt his watchful gaze on her and breathed a sigh of relief when she heard his murmur. "Let's get you home, then."

Supremely aware of his body on their jog home, Cassie continually forced her eyes to the streetlights along the way. With no conversation to distract her, she heard his breath, the pounding of his feet on the pavement. She could practically feel the flex and stretch of his muscles, and the feeling brought images of Joshua's naked body flexing and stretching over her own. Cassie shook her head at her distracting thoughts and wryly admitted to herself that a cold shower would probably be in order at this rate.

Still, Joshua hadn't pressed her about Billy Joe. And he'd taken up for her last night when Billy Joe had gotten nasty. For some strange reason she couldn't begin to understand, Cassie felt she owed him an answer to his earlier question—not necessarily a wrenching spill-your-guts disclosure, just a simple explanation. Cassie laughed inwardly, as if there were a simple explanation.

When they reached her door, Cassie turned to him. "Thanks for the run, Joshua." She smiled. "Although my muscles won't be thanking me tomorrow."

Twirling her key ring around her finger, she took a deep breath, but didn't look at him. "About Billy Joe . . . we were engaged when I was nineteen. He eloped with another girl one day before our wedding."

She felt his hand on her shoulder and looked up to find a confused expression on his face which, coupled with his next question, oddly pleased her.

"Why would he do that?"

She hadn't intended to tell him any more, but decided she'd satisfy both of their curiosities. Wondering how he'd respond, she looked him straight in the eye and enunciated each word carefully.

"She was pregnant."

SEVEN

Joshua stared at the door Cassie had closed on him and considered the symbolism of her gesture. She'd watched his face for a fleeting moment, murmured good night, and closed the door. He'd always believed he had a pretty tough skin, but her continued efforts to get rid of him were starting to wear a little.

After she dropped that bomb about her ex-fiance, he'd been so stunned he'd just stood there saying nothing, still gaping at the sight of her closed door after two full minutes. That last punchline revealed quite a bit about why Cassie was so elusive when it came to serious involvement. The lady had been burned. He toyed with the idea of knocking on her door and insisting they finish this conversation, but decided against it.

She needed to be alone. And he needed some time to assimilate this latest bit of information; time to see where this piece of the Cassandra Warner puzzle fit.

For that matter, he needed to figure out his own feelings. He still wanted to make love to her. When he'd seen her long, bare legs and lucious figure so temptingly wrapped in skimpy shorts and tank top, it had taken every bit of his control not to scoop her up and suggest that they get their workout on her bed. Yes, he wanted her, badly, and he had the ache to prove it.

Joshua glanced thoughtfully at the door a moment longer and turned to run home, resolving that Cassie couldn't shut him out forever. Her desire for him was evident; so, it was just a matter of time. Oddly, he wanted more than desire from her. But then beggars couldn't be choosers.

On the other side of the door, Cassie breathed a sigh of relief when she saw that Joshua had left. A blank expression had crossed over his features, and she found she just couldn't wait to see that expression change to one of pity.

She felt a strange mixture of relief, disappointment, and arousal. Darn that man! She'd been aware of every move of his gorgeous body, and he hadn't seemed to look at her unless it was with solicitous concern. And why should she care if he didn't want her anymore? For Pete's sake, isn't that what she'd been working for?

Not liking the surge of disappointment, Cassie groaned and headed for the bathroom, stripping off her clothes with jerky movements as she deliberated over what temperature of water to use. Hot for her overworked muscles, or cold because of Joshua.

The next morning, Cassie smiled ruefully when she watched Maggie gape at her as she politely allowed one of Joshua's contractors in to take measurements for new carpet.

"Landsakes, Cassie, what's come over you? You've thrown every other contractor out on his ear." Maggie smacked her gum furiously, waiting for her boss's response.

"I think I'm just facing reality, Maggie. Joshua Daniels is going to move his printing company into this building in a couple of months, and there's not a thing I can do to change it." She sighed and tossed her realtor's card onto the counter. "The best thing that I can do is find another place for my store."

"But you've already looked," Maggie insisted.

"Yes, but I haven't found anything." Cassie took a deep breath and stiffened her spine. "I'm not giving up. My realtor is taking me out on Saturday again, and she'll call if she discovers anything before then." She almost thumped her fist on the counter for emphasis.

Maggie smiled at Cassie's determination. "Well, you'll not have me doubting you. You've accomplished quite a bit for a young woman your age." Her brows knitted thoughtfully. "The only thing missing is a good man in your life. If Joshua Daniels wasn't kicking us out, I'd place bets on him. That man has it bad for you."

Cassie groaned and thought, *And I've got it bad for him, but that isn't helping me with my shop.*

Fortunately, the bell tinkled, signalling the arrival of another customer and allowing Cassie to withhold comment.

Kim breezed in at lunchtime and shared a sub sandwich with Cassie. Cassie grinned at the nervous energy emanating from her petite friend.

With her leg swinging back and forth, Kim slit her

eyes at Cassie. "I've plied you with food and diet cola. Fred gave me the scoop on the scene at Joe's the other night. Are you gonna fill me in on all the juicy details or just leave it to my torrid imagination?"

Cassie rolled her eyes and shook her head. "Well, Kim, I have to admire your approach, but if you heard that Billy Joe insulted me and Joshua punched him out and I ran out, then you pretty much got the gist of it."

"Who's Billy Joe? What did he say? It must have been pretty bad for Joshua to hit him." Kim paused thoughtfully. "I mean, I've heard he had his share of scrapes in high school, but I haven't ever seen him hit anyone before." Kim's eyes sparkled with excitement as she grinned broadly. "Oh, isn't it exciting? Having another man defend your honor."

"No, it wasn't exciting. It was humiliating." Cassie stood and thrust her hair behind her ear in frustration. "Kim, you know how I hate scenes. Now, how can I walk back into that restaurant without feeling like everyone's staring at me and whispering?"

"I guess you've got a point," Kim said sympathetically. "I was hoping this might have patched things up between you and Joshua. Not so, huh?"

Cassie shook her head. "He was very nice, but he still refuses to extend my lease."

"Hmmm." Kim uncrossed her legs and stood abruptly. "The other reason that I came to see you was to invite you to my parents' place tonight. They're out of town and they've got a pool, so—" Kim held up a hand as Cassie opened her mouth in refusal. "Just listen first. I thought I'd have you and Marie over for pizza and swimming tonight. No men. And we won't say a word about your unfortunate experience at Joe's. We'll discuss important things like fashion, food, and when we should buy our tickets for the Chippendale dancers.''

Laughing, Cassie considered her bubbly friend's invitation and decided she could use an evening of light conversation and feminine companionship. Between her problems with the store and the scene at Joe's, she'd felt the weight of the world on her shoulders. "Okay, you've sold me. Give me the time and the place and I'll come, complete with bikini.''

"Seven o'clock and let me write the address for you.'' Kim scribbled the address on a notepad, and studied Cassie. "You won't back out, will you? I mean, we'll be counting on you.''

Cassie noticed a strange glint in Kim's eye and wondered about it. When she couldn't figure it out, she placed her hand over her heart and said solemnly, "I promise to be there at seven.''

"Don't back out,'' Kim admonished and whirled out the door.

Joshua finished his last lap and drew a deep breath of air. After grabbing the raft, he pushed himself up on it and sank back in total relaxation. A sigh of contentment escaped his lips. *This is the life,* he thought. Kim was nice to lend out her parents' pool to the guys for the night. Fred and Jack would be back with the pizza and beer any minute. This was just what he needed—a night out with the guys, with no sign of the female sex. Cassie had him so tied up in knots he didn't know what to do. She even had him regretting the fact that he'd bought her building and would be moving into it soon with his own business.

He squinted his eyes shut tightly. *No,* he admonished himself, *he wouldn't think of her tonight.* He'd just relax and be with the guys. Then, he jumped as he heard a familiar female voice. Oh, Lord, now he was hearing things.

"Kim, Marie," Cassie called out and lifted her T-shirt over her head, eagerly looking forward to a relaxing dip in the pool. She unlocked the gate and ran to the patio.

Then, she gasped at the sight of Joshua reclining on a float in the pool.

Joshua stared at the shapely, scantily clad beauty standing before him. He blinked and groaned. Now, he was having delusions. That could not be Cassie standing before him dressed in a black string bikini.

"Joshua Daniels, what are you doing in Kim's pool?" she asked furiously.

Joshua blinked again. The vision talked. Maybe she was real after all.

"Well, I'm waiting." She crossed her arms over her chest in defiance.

"I could ask you the same thing." He slid off the float and walked forward, leaning his forearms on the side of the pool. "Fred and Jack dropped me off here while they went to get their swim trunks and a pizza." He glanced at his waterproof watch. "As a matter-of-fact, they should be here about now."

"Fred and Jack?" she repeated in confusion and turned as she heard a vehicle pull into the driveway.

A young man hurried through the gate and called out, "Pizza and beer for Cassie Warner and Joshua Daniels. It's already paid for." The delivery boy stopped abruptly when he caught sight of Cassie. His mouth gaped open "Ah, ah, are you," his Adam's apple bobbled, "Cassie Warner?"

Joshua could appreciate the boy's bemusement. Cassie was a sight to behold in her present state, and for some reason he didn't want to share her with anyone else. He stepped forward to take the pizza and beer, and slipped the guy a buck he found in his slacks' pocket. "I'm Joshua Daniels. Have you got anything else, like an explanation?"

The young man forced his attention to Joshua and nodded. "Yeah, there's a note taped to the top of the box." He looked back at Cassie soulfully. "Is there anything else—"

"Not a thing," Joshua said cheerfully and went to open the gate. He was going to have to mop up the drool if he didn't get that kid out of here. "Thanks for everything," Joshua said as he watched the delivery boy's reluctant departure.

The gate closed with a bang, and Joshua pointed to the pizza box he'd placed on the patio table. "Read it to me. I don't think my eyes can handle any more surprises tonight."

Cassie looked at him blankly and then did as he asked. " 'Cassie and Joshua, please come to terms. You're driving everybody crazy, including yourselves. Put us out of our misery and make peace with each other.' It's signed, 'Your caring friends, Jack, Fred, Marie, and Kim.' " She balled up the paper and threw it. "I should have known she was up to something. Kim practically made me swear that I would come tonight. 'Just us girls,' she said. My Aunt Fanny."

Joshua hid his inward grin at the picture she made.

her flaring temper brought a flush to her cheeks that, as he looked closer, extended to her whole body for that matter. Sympathizing with her distress, he said, "If it makes you feel any better, remember that you've still got transportation out of here. I got dumped like yesterday's laundry."

Looking up as Joshua's gaze skated over her body, she suddenly remembered her lack of clothing and blushed furiously. She turned and murmured, "Where did I put my T-shirt?"

She could hear the grin in his voice when he thrust the missing shirt in front of her averted gaze. "Is this what you're looking for? Don't feel you have to cover up on my account. I'm not the least bit offended by your attire."

She snatched it from him and pulled it over her head eyeing him balefully. "So, what do we do now?"

Now, that's a leading question, Joshua thought. *Play it cool, Daniels. Not only have you got her all alone and half-dressed, but she's also your only ride out of this place.* He strode over to the patio table and gestured toward the food. "Well, we've got a hot pizza and cold beer that are gonna turn into cold pizza and warm beer if we don't go ahead and eat it. I say, we eat it."

Chewing her lip thoughtfully, Cassie considered leaving or eating, and when her stomach rumbled, she decided quickly on eating and then leaving. Besides, since he seemed more interested in his stomach right now, he probably wouldn't present a threat to her. Although, standing there with his back to her in his little blue swim trunks, Cassie had to confess that the rear view of Joshua was almost as good as the front.

She shook her head at her wayward thoughts, then clapped her hands together and said crisply, "I agree. Let's eat. What's on the pizza?"

Joshua grinned and through open the box with a flourish. "Everything!"

She pursed her lips momentarily and then smiled in satisfaction. "Except anchovies."

Laughing, he pulled out a chair for her and handed her a slice of the pizza. Then, he popped the top on a beer and set it next to her on the table.

"Thank you. This is delicious," she said between bites. "Though I could kill them for setting us up, I have to admit I appreciate the food."

Joshua licked his thumb and raised an eyebrow. "But not the company?"

She could have kicked herself for sounding so rude when he was obviously trying to make the best of the situation. "No, I didn't mean it that way. I just wasn't expecting you . . . and I don't like feeling tricked . . . and—"

He laughed and waved aside her awkward explanation. "That's okay, Cassie. I was looking forward to a nice peaceful night out with the guys myself."

Feeling put in her place with that remark, she started on another piece of pizza. She watched him turn on the radio, and shook her head when he offered her another beer. Her gaze fell helplessly over his male contours, and she couldn't find a single part of him that wasn't pleasing to her. From his dark hair attractively mussed and not quite dry from his swim, his broad shoulders and muscular chest, flat stomach, and powerful thighs all the way down to his feet. His feet, Cassie stared at them, she'd never really looked at his feet before.

Large, but nicely shaped like the rest of him; masculine looking.

"Is something wrong with my feet?"

His deep voice penetrated her survey of his body and she felt her cheeks heat. What was she supposed to say now? Oh, not a thing, Joshua. As a matter-of-fact, I was just admiring them along with the rest of you. "Uh, nothing. Uh, I was just looking at the concrete." She turned her head and groaned at her lack of originality.

"Yeah, well, if you're into concrete, I'm sure it's interesting," he said skeptically. He wiped off his mouth with a napkin and stood. "Do you want to swim?"

Incredulous at his suggestion, she stared at him. "You've got to be kidding. I just crammed down three huge pieces of pizza and you're suggesting a swim. I'll sink!"

He clasped her hand in his and pulled her up. "No, you won't. You would have swum if Kim and Marie were here. You don't have to do a lot of laps. The water's great. It'll relax you." He plucked up another napkin and gently rubbed it across her lips, and Cassie felt as if he'd burned her with the innocent gesture. She looked into his eyes and saw that he had felt the heat between them. A light of desire flared in his eyes until he released her hand and turned away.

"Look, I'll go in first just to prove to you that the temperature's comfortable." Joshua knew he was doing everything in his power to keep her there, short of chaining her, and wondered when he'd last worked so hard to get a woman to go swimming with him. Still, he couldn't sit at that table one minute longer. She'd been practically devouring him with her eyes and it was having a hellish effect on his already reduced self-control. What he'd really like to do to Cassie Warner involved dispensing with that man-trapping bathing suit of hers and showing her just what kind of effect she had on him.

Hell! Maybe the water would help. With that thought, he dove into the pool.

Watching Joshua's splash into the inviting water, Cassie deliberated over joining him, and sighed. Why did she find it necessary to belabor every move she made when she was with Joshua? Impatient with her efforts to distance herself from him, Cassie impulsively stripped off her T-shirt. She was here with a darned good-looking and charming man, and although she knew there was no future for Joshua and herself, Cassie decided it was about time she had some fun.

Smiling with glee, she ran to the pool and executed a perfect cannonball.

"Marco," Cassie called.

"Polo," Joshua answered and laughed as she drew nearer.

"Marco," she repeated.

"Polo, oh, you got me!" he said as her arms enfolded him, and her eyes flew open from their previously blinded state.

After thirty minutes of splashing and three games of Marco Polo, Joshua shook his head in wonder at the uninhibited water sprite with whom he was sharing the pool. He'd never glimpsed this side of her personality and, as with just about everything else he'd learned about her, he was entranced all over again.

He felt pole-axed.

She'd teased and played and splashed so freely that now that she was in his arms, as he'd fantasized earlier, he almost didn't know what to do next. Almost.

When he saw her aqua eyes darken and watched her gaze fall admiringly to his chest, he tightened his arms around her and took her lips in a searching kiss.

Cassie closed her eyes and concentrated solely on the sense of touch. His mouth was firm and tender on hers, and the faint rasp of his rough face felt delicious against her skin. She backed away briefly for air, then with parted lips sought his mouth again. Banishing her tendency to play it safe, Cassie pressed herself closer to him and enjoyed the feel of his bare chest rubbing against her scantily-clad upper body. His response was instantaneous and flattering. With a quick intake of breath, he tightened his arms around her. He drove his tongue into the silken depths, drawing out her heated response.

White hot fire licked through her veins as he clasped her hips against his masculinity, showing her in unmistakable terms how much he desired her. A tiny warning light flickered in the back of her mind, but she quickly rejected it in favor of Joshua's sensual assault on her senses. Besides, she'd decided not to over think tonight. And with the ache he'd started in her, the only thing on her mind was Joshua.

Joshua reluctantly pulled his mouth from Cassie's tempting lips and held her tightly against his pounding heart. His labored breathing and arousal made his voice husky with desire. "Cassie, we've got to stop, or I'm not going to be able to. I'm probably gonna kick myself for saying this, but I can't take any more cold showers. If you want to stop, tell me now, cause the only thing on my mind right now is getting rid of these bathing suits and getting as close as two people can possibly get."

Unbearably aroused by his words, Cassie pulled her head back to look him in the eye. Even with his nostrils flared and his eyes glazed with passion, he was still giving her an opportunity to quit. Only this time, she didn't want to quit. The mere suggestion of his hardened masculinity pressing against that aching part of her sent her into flames, and she found she could deny neither Joshua nor herself any more.

She leaned forward until her lips were a breath from his and whispered, "What if I don't want to stop?" When she felt him stiffen, she tamped down her feeling of inadequacy and gave it her best shot.

"What if I want to get rid of these bathing suits, too?"

Joshua was sure his heart had stopped beating. Only in his dreams had Cassie ever done something like this. He had to be certain, so he asked her, "Are you sure?"

And when she nodded, he remembered to breathe and loosened the tie to the top of her bikini.

Cassie couldn't stand his intent stare and turned her head. After baring herself in more ways than one, she wondered if she was up to snuff.

"You're beautiful," he said, moving her over to the graduated steps in the shallow end of the pool. The water beaded over the creamy expanse of her rounded breasts and rosy peaks, and he brushed his lips over the top of her feminine curves, licking a drop of moisture off each one. She moaned in response, longing for him to feed on her aching nipples.

"Tell me what you want."

"Kiss me." Digging her fingers into the hair of his lowered head, she murmured, "Yes. Oh, there."

Joshua sat down on a step and pulled her between his powerful thighs. He kissed her beaded tips and then drew one into his mouth sucking firmly, wringing a pleasure pain that travelled to her feminine core. Then, as he gave the same preferred treatment to her other aching nipple, he massaged the breast his mouth had just left.

Cassie grew restless under his ministrations and ran her hands feverishly over his shoulders and back. "Let me touch you."

After one last, adoring kiss, Joshua brought her into his lap and nuzzled her ear. She sighed at the gesture and brought her restless hands to his masculine chest. The texture of the damp, curly hair entranced her and she ran her tongue lightly over each of his masculine nipples. She heard him catch his breath and looked up uncertainly.

"I liked it," he said as if reading her mind. "I just can't stand but so much of it."

Cassie smiled shyly and continued her exploration of his muscled frame. She ran a finger lightly across his flat belly and felt a tremor run through him. In awe of her power over this tremendous man, she put her hand below the water and skimmed the top of his bathing suit.

He pulled her hand away and held it to his lips. "Too much more of that and we won't make it to the bed.'' He licked each finger and Cassie turned to liquid beneath his hot gaze.

''I don't want to wait.''

Joshua shuddered. ''Cassie, we can't.''

''Why not?'' she asked, shaky with her desire for him.

''I didn't bring any . . . protection.'' His voice was husky.

''I'm on the pill,'' she countered in a breathy voice.

His eyes darkened as he studied her. ''Here?'' She bit her lip as he tasted her palm with his tongue.

''Here.''

He stood up and allowed her to lean against him as he shoved off his bathing suit. Cassie's eyes widened at the sight of his full arousal and felt the ache intensify between her thighs. After he sat back down in the water and pulled her into his lap, he untied the soggy strings at each of her hips with agonizing slowness. He held her gaze as the material floated away and his hand found her nest of femininity. Her languid, passion-filled eyes were trapped by his until he ran his thumb over the pearl of sensitivity. She moaned and dropped her head forward.

''Oh, Joshua.'' She breathed his name and felt the rest of the world fade as pleasure overrode everything else. Pleasure and the desire to have him inside her. Instinctively, she reached down to touch his hardened manhood, and he gasped.

Once again, he pulled her hand away and she made a sound of frustration. He shifted her body over his and nudged her head up with a gentle nuzzle from his chin. ''Look at me,'' he ordered roughly.

And as she gazed up at his dark, possessive eyes, he

settled her hips on top of him and slowly penetrated her waiting femininity. They stayed that way for a long moment and Cassie stared in wonder at the beauty of the moment.

With long, smooth strokes, Joshua set the rhythm for her escalating tension and when he moved his hand down to stroke her, she cried out and felt as if she were bursting into tiny pieces. She tightened around him and with a final thrust, Joshua groaned his completion.

Quivering with the aftershocks of her release, she slumped against him with her arms wrapped around his neck. She was so overwhelmed with her physical and emotional response that a trickle of tears ran down her face.

Joshua cupped her chin in his hand and anxiously studied her. "You're crying. Did I hurt you?"

"No-o-o." She shook her head and swallowed hard. "It's just never been this wonderful for me before. I thought I might be . . ." Blushing, her voice trailed off.

His eyes narrowed, but his touch was tender as he gently wiped the tears away with his thumb. "You thought you might be what?"

She turned her head away and answered in a low voice, "Frigid." Cassie cringed at the silence. Perhaps the pleasure had been mostly one-sided. Joshua had seemed to enjoy their lovemaking, but what did she know? It wasn't as if she was vastly experienced.

Joshua finally responded with shocked tones. "You are kidding me, aren't you?" He sighed when she didn't answer. "Look at me. Cassie, I don't know where you got the idea that you're frigid. Hell, if you'd been any hotter, we'd have both gone up in flames, pool or no pool."

She looked at his dark, intense eyes and smiled shyly. "Then you're not disappointed?"

"No," he answered seriously, "but I will be if you don't come home with me tonight."

Cassie had already burned one of the bridges connecting her with the unhappy part of her past. And there were still others that would have to be dealt with, but not tonight. Tonight was for Joshua. "Will you drive?"

An hour later, Cassie lay on his big bed with her head on Joshua's shoulder, and her body curled into his. Part of her wondered if she had lost her mind, part of her was sure she had lost her mind. But the biggest part of her simply didn't care because she felt so wonderful.

Turning her head, she studied his shadowed jaw and brushed her fingers across the rough stubble. At her touch, he took her hand and kissed it.

"I was just trying to figure out when I started wanting you," Joshua said in a deep voice. Then, he grinned and she traced the crinkles at the corners of his eyes. "At first, I thought it was when we danced at the wedding. Then, I figured it was after I heard a few wild tales from Fred and Jack about you at the rehearsal. But, I think it was when I saw you in the grocery store with your shredded hose, trying desperately to get out of the date we won."

"What wild tales?" she asked.

"Hmmm?"

She removed her hand from his face and asked again,

"What wild tales did Fred and Jack tell you about me?"

"Nothing that wild," he said, brushing aside her question.

Cassie moved away from him. "You distinctly said wild. Now, the least you can do is explain yourself."

With an exaggerated sigh, he relented, "Okay, but only if you move back over here."

She settled back in and waited expectantly.

"Fred and Jack told me you have a very annoying habit. Apparently, after you went out with them a few times and they started trying to get a little more serious, you set them up with Kim and Marie."

She was dumbfounded. "You know, I never really thought that much about it. Jack and Fred were very nice, but I never wanted anything serious with them. And Kim always talked about how cute she thought Fred was. Well, it just seemed natural to . . . kind of help them get together." She paused. "Did they really think that I did it intentionally? Like some kind of game?"

Joshua laughed at her distress and hugged her. "I got the impression that they thought it was pretty fishy that you set both of them up with two of your best friends. I was glad they warned me about your little habit, just in case you decided to use the same ruse on me."

"I guess you're right. I didn't plan it; it just seemed so logical for Jack and Fred to hook up with Kim and Marie. But I couldn't seem to find another acceptable woman for you." She turned to him and smiled. "I have to confess to being glad that I'm the one in your arms tonight and not anyone else."

"That makes two of us." Joshua kissed her upturned lips. Torn between making love to Cassie again and clearing up the issue of Billy Joe, Joshua groaned at the sight of her. Her silky skin was an ivory pink, her swollen lips an open invitation, and her eyes glowed with a sensuality he was sure she hadn't known she'd possessed. He sighed and looked away briefly to regain his control.

"There's one more thing, Cassie." Joshua hesitated. "The other night after you told me why Billy Joe had eloped with someone else, you left before I had a chance to say anything." He watched her cheeks turn pink, and she cast her eyes downward. "Please don't look away. I'm not saying this to embarrass you." Running his thumbs along her delicate jawline, he continued, "I just wanted you to know that I can imagine how some of that may have felt for you." He watched her eyes widen in disbelief and grinned ruefully. "Yeah, humiliation's a pretty common human experience. I was out with a couple of friends from high school when my natural father showed up drunk and talking crazy. I was so embarrassed that I avoided those guys like they were the plague. It was silly, but I was scared to death that they would spread it all over school that Joshua Daniels's real dad was a smelly old drunk." He gave her nose a butterfly kiss and took in her expression of compassion, and finished briskly. "Anyway, I'm sorry Billy Joe humiliated you, but I'm damn glad he didn't marry you. Because you've given me the most magnificent night of my life, pretty lady, and the time on that clock, along with other things, tells me this night has just begun."

Then Joshua lowered his lips to hers and Cassie

began a magical journey of learning the power and pleasure of her stored up sensuality, because this man with
the caring chocolate-brown eyes seemed to have the
key to unlock the door.

EIGHT

Cassie opened her eyes, shut them, then she opened them again. She was lying on her side, pressed intimately against Joshua. His hand rested possessively over her hip, and she was dressed in . . . nothing. Then she remembered how they'd spent the night making love over and over again, and almost groaned out loud.

It had been a perfect night, and Joshua had been a perfect lover, and she was going to make a perfect fool of herself if she didn't get herself out of his bed. What do people do on the morning after, anyway?

She'd known that last night seemed especially set aside for the two of them. But she'd also known that it wouldn't last past the night. There was still the issue of her shop between them, and even though Cassie had given herself physically to Joshua, she knew she wasn't ready for a serious relationship. Besides, if she was going to save her business, she didn't need any other distractions in her life.

And to say that Joshua Daniels had the ability to distract her was putting it mildly, she thought with a wry smile. Even now, she found it nearly irresistible to dip her tongue into that cleft chin of his. He was sexy awake. But sleeping, he wore a tousled, debauched look that made her fairly preen with feminine pride.

Cassie craned her neck and noted the time. Six-fifteen. She needed to get out of his bed and retrieve her bathing suit. With a final longing glance at the handsome man sprawled beside her, she eased herself inch by careful inch out of his bed. At one point, she was sure she'd blown it. When she lifted Joshua's hand from her hip, he tossed restlessly and she held her breath. Uneasily, she released it and scrambled away.

Finding her bathing suit was easy; Joshua had removed it immediately upon their entrance into his apartment. But, the keys were another matter. Where did he put the keys? With Joshua occupying her with sensuous kisses and erotic touches as he removed her clothes the night before, she wouldn't have cared if he'd thrown them out the window. She checked the kitchen counter, the coffee table, even the bathroom. Then, the phone rang and Cassie froze and stared at the intrusive instrument.

Who would be calling Joshua at this time in the morning? she wondered. She breathed a sigh of relief when the ringing stopped and the answering machine came on. Just as she spied her keys sitting next to the phone, the caller's voice sounded. "Joshua, this is Ken Blomburg. Listen, try a little harder to get our tenant moved out of our building. I just got a call from our supplier and he's gonna be able to get us the equipment sooner than we planned. Call me back with the results.''

Cassie struggled to ignore the lump in her throat as she quietly closed the door and ran to her car.

Stomping through the apartment, Joshua called out Cassie's name repeatedly. She was nowhere to be found. He let out a frustrated roar and headed toward the phone. A tiny hope rose within him at the sight of the blinking message light on his answering machine and he eagerly pressed the button to play the message.

He smiled fondly. Perhaps she was a bit shy after having been such a vixen in bed last night. It was possible that she felt awkward about the morning after and had left an affectionate message for him instead. He could tell she wasn't widely experienced by her initial modesty. But after Cassie had shed her inhibitions, she'd turned into a tigress. He grew aroused just remembering how hot and tight she'd felt.

Joshua cursed and fiercely rubbed his whiskered face when he heard his partner's voice and message. Sorely tempted to rip the answering machine out of the wall, he uttered another colorful obscenity and trudged off to the shower. Miss Cassandra Warner had a few more lessons to learn about Joshua Daniels.

She hadn't called and there was no way in hell he was letting her walk out free and clear after last night.

"No way," said Joshua with gritty determination as he turned the shower on full force.

Twenty minutes later, after two cups of coffee, Joshua felt in a better frame of mind to approach the new day. He decided to give Cassie a little space and see her later in the day.

He answered the phone after the first ring, and felt his stomach sink like lead to his feet.

"Vandalized?" Joshua repeated to the police officer.

He thought of Cassie's store and clenched his fist. "When did this happen? Was anyone injured?" He spat out the questions in machine-gun fashion, and felt a wave of relief when he learned that no one had been at the shop when it was vandalized.

"Is Cassie Warner there? How is she?"

The officer assured him that Miss Warner appeared upset, but composed, and Joshua told the man that he would leave for the store immediately. Joshua grabbed his jacket and dashed out the door.

Cassie felt her hands tremble as she picked up another doll that had been destroyed and willed her hands to be still. She had to control herself. Everything seemed to be coming down around her. This shop that had been such a crucial part in rebuilding her self-esteem, and life had been at risk since Joshua had bought her building.

Now, it was destroyed.

Shaking her head at the meaninglessness of it, she gazed around the room. It looked similar to that of the dress shop after its desecration. Paint and motor oil had been spilled and thrown everywhere. How could she possibly rebuild? Many of her orders were placed months in advance. Local craftsmen provided some of her inventory, but the majority of it was secured through specialty companies. They'd even gotten to her office. They had broken through the door, ravaged through her papers, and dumped her plants on the floor.

She heard a strong, masculine voice. Cassie looked

up and felt her veneer of control start to shatter as Joshua carried on an intense conversation with the police officer. Part of her wanted to fling herself into his strong arms for comfort, and part of her wanted to scream at him to get out of her store and her life. It seemed that everything had gone wrong for her since Joshua had walked into her life.

Everything except last night.

And Cassie seriously questioned the wisdom of her actions the previous evening.

Dispassionately, she figured Joshua might be sorry that her merchandise had been destroyed, but he'd probably be immensely relieved that she'd have to move her store from his property. Then, he would be able to get on with building his own successful business, with her out of the way. Momentarily, she wondered if his interest in her would wane now that the way was free and clear for him to move in.

At that thought, her throat clogged with emotion and she cursed herself for her attraction to him. Even now, her eyes were helplessly drawn to his tall, imposing figure as he walked steadily toward her.

Cassie stiffened at the consoling hand he placed on her shoulder.

"Cassie," he said, genuinely contrite, "this is such a mess. I'm so sorry."

Backing away, she held her head high, unable to see the bright, unshed tears in her eyes that revealed her true emotion. "Yes, it is a mess. I'll have it cleared up as soon as possible."

"Well, of course, you will," he agreed. "We'll get a cleaning crew out here first thing."

Cassie's heart sank. Joshua's primary concern was

sweeping out her store and her mess so that he could move ahead. She tossed her hair and assumed a defiant stance. Far be it for her to stand in the way of progress. She was no dummy. She knew when she had lost.

"Joshua," Cassie said coldly, "I realize that you're very eager to set up your own store, and this unfortunate incident has just made it very easy for you to get rid of me, but it may take me a few days to determine what I can salvage."

She bit her lip to keep it from quivering and felt the sting of tears in her eyes. Her voice shook with suppressed emotion. "You may think that it looks like a bunch of junk, but this represents the last three years of my life."

Joshua snatched her tensely held hands and gave an exclamation of disbelief. "You don't really believe I'm thinking of moving my equipment in here at a time like this."

"Oh, come off it, Joshua." She ripped her hands away from him, her eyes shooting off sparks of anger. "The game's over. I heard your business partner's message right before I left your apartment this morning. I'm sure he'll get a good laugh when you tell him about your methods of persuasion."

She crossed her arms over her chest. "I wonder if it fed your immense ego to know how little experience I had. Well, it looks as if you got your way all the way around. You had me in bed and you're getting your property even sooner than you'd hoped. I'll be out of here as soon as I can. Just leave me alone."

Joshua grasped her arm and jerked her against his chest. Cassie could see by the tight jaw and narrowed eyes that he was livid with anger. His voice was low and deadly cold. "You talk a lot of nonsense when you're pushed into a corner, pretty lady. I'm not going to hold you responsible for the things you just said, because I figure you're having a hard enough time not getting completely hysterical. But I will correct a few things. One, I have never tried to get you into bed to persuade you to move out of the store sooner. Two, if it fed my ego to take you to bed last night, then you could have gotten a whole day's nourishment on what last night did for your ego. I left you with no doubt as to how you affected me. At least I didn't sneak out the back door."

Cassie cringed at his words and started to protest.

"Finally," he continued mercilessly, "I'll leave you alone for now, because, quite frankly, I'm tempted to wring your little neck."

He loosed her roughly, and ground out his parting statement. "We'll finish this later."

Cassie sank to her knees and covered her head in confusion as he left. Although she'd remained remarkably composed throughout the ordeal, she felt the tears cover her face as her emotions snapped beyond her control. It was just too much. Last night with Joshua, his partner's message on the answering machine, the vandalism, and now she'd said all those terrible things to him. She didn't know what to believe.

Sniffing, she removed a tissue from her skirt pocket and blew her nose and looked around. Well, she couldn't figure out everything right now, but she could sift through the remains of her inventory. The store had always been a source of strength for her and even in its present condition, she clutched at the idea of it as if it were a lifeline.

Cassie made her plans and put them into action immediately. She wanted to be alone in her store, she simply couldn't handle any more questions, so she called Maggie and told her to stay home the rest of the day. Initially, the older woman insisted on coming, but Cassie refused and promised Maggie she could come tomorrow. After thanking the police officers, she shooed them on their way and rolled up her sleeves.

Luckily, she still had several empty boxes in the back room. She pulled them out and began the arduous task of separating the merchandise into two piles; that which was destroyed and that which could be salvaged.

After several hours, Cassie saw that the destroyed merchandise pile was much larger than the salvageable pile. She gazed at the clock and noted that it was well past lunchtime and decided to take a break. After receiving a visit from her insurance agent, she brought a fast-food meal back to the store and began working again.

Time and time again, Joshua's face floated across her mind as she worked and Cassie agonized over the words they'd exchanged this morning. Perhaps she was wrong, perhaps Joshua wasn't trying to finagle her out of the store. After all, he hadn't broached the subject with her in weeks. Her head throbbed from the strain of the day. She noticed the other shops closing up for the night and started loading the salvageable merchandise into boxes. The vandals had broken the glass door to gain entry and she had no desire to remain there alone after dark.

She collected her purse, headed for the door, and gave a little start when she saw Joshua standing there with a man in work clothes. She searched his eyes and found an unreadable expression on his face as he surveyed the room.

"Cassie, this is Mr. Parker. He's going to repair the glass in the door and I'll be having a security alarm that hooks up to the police department installed tomorrow."

"Oh." She paused, then said, "Thanks."

He shoved his hands into his pockets and looked around the room again. "Looks like you got a lot done today. Did you have someone helping you?"

Cassie felt awkward because she still couldn't read his mood. Her eyes drank in the sight of him—his tousled dark hair, tired brooding eyes, loosened tie and pushed-up sleeves. He looked great. But then, Cassie was finding that Joshua looked great to her anytime. Twisting her hair nervously, she answered his question. "Uh, no. Maggie's coming tomorrow." When he didn't respond, she breathlessly hurried on, "I should be out in a few days."

Her breath caught at the pained expression on his face. Her heart beat wildly when he moved closer to her and took her hand. He glanced over his shoulder at the workman, then pulled her to the back of the store.

His eyes searched hers as he whispered, "Do you really think I took you to bed to get you out of this store?"

Cassie covered her forehead with a shaky hand and choked out her response. "Oh, Joshua, I don't know. Last night was wonderful, but I panicked when I woke up this morning. Then, when I heard your partner's message, I felt like I'd been suckered all over again." She glanced back at him and felt like wailing. "I'm so confused and tired."

Joshua's arms enfolded her and Cassie sighed at the

strength he emanated. She could use some strong loving arms around her after the day she'd had.

"Come on," he murmured in a deep voice. "I'm taking you home."

His breath fluttered against her hair, his male scent teased her nostrils, and she was so tempted. "I can't. I've got my car."

"I'll send someone out for it later. Cassie, please. Let me do this for you."

She looked back into his face and saw the sincerity and concern and something she couldn't quite name glowing from his eyes. She felt weak as a kitten from the emotional stress of the day. No match for the strength he exuded or the spell he seemed to have cast over her, she whispered her acquiescence. "Take me home."

And he took her to his home.

Later, when she rested on his sofa, she smiled as he pulled off her shoes and rested them on the coffee table. "I still don't understand why you didn't take me to my house," she protested weakly.

"Because," he said patiently, "I don't want you to be disturbed by phone calls from a bunch of nosy people. I'll turn the volume down on my phone and you can get a good night's rest here." He looked at her drooping eyelids and smiled indulgently. "Besides, you don't look as if you could make it to bed, let alone fix yourself anything to eat."

"Some of those nosy callers could be my best friends."

Joshua shrugged. "I'll give Kim a call and tell her to pass the word that you're not available for the evening." He gazed at her with determination. "I'm going to start your bath water. Can you take off your clothes yourself, or do you need some help?''

Cassie's eyes flew wide open at the question and she sputtered, "I—I—I think I can undress myself.''

"Fine," Joshua answered mildly as he left the room. "You can use my robe. It's hanging on the back of the bedroom door.''

Although her rubbery legs barely carried her, she stripped off her clothes and wondered how she'd gotten into this situation. Did Joshua expect them to sleep together again tonight? True, the idea was exciting even to her tired body, but she didn't know if she could handle that much intimacy in her present state. She supposed she'd better broach the subject before he got too far ahead in his plans. She knotted the long terry robe and went into the bathroom.

"Sorry, I don't have any bubbles," he said as she entered the small room.

"Oh," she said, "that's okay. Uh, Joshua," she hesitated and felt the color rise to her cheeks. He waited expectantly and Cassie cursed her inexperience. Was there any way to put this delicately? "Uh, I'm really tired tonight. I mean, you weren't expecting . . ." Her voice trailed off.

To her consternation, Joshua laughed. Loudly.

"Oh, Cassie," he said, subduing his mirth at her indignant expression. "Let me relieve your mind. As much as I want to make love to you again, I realize that you're not exactly in a state of mind or body conducive to lovemaking." He squeezed her arm lightly. "So, just relax. The big bad wolf won't get you tonight.''

After a luxurious soak in the tub and a bowl of soup

with crackers, Cassie pulled Joshua's T-shirt over her head and sank into his bed. She curled into a little ball and wondered why the bed seemed so large. Joshua assured her he would take the couch, yet she found herself wishing he'd drop his chivalry just long enough to hold her through the night.

She let out a little sigh and hugged the extra pillow to her as her eyes drooped. Perhaps, if she closed her eyes, the scent of him on the bed linens would be enough.

After Joshua made a few phone calls to Kim, his business partner, and his realtor, he peeked in on Cassie. She made an arresting picture with her silky blonde hair tousled over the pillow, her delicate eyelashes and flushed cheeks. One hand was stretched over her head in unconscious sensual invitation, and Joshua felt a pleasurable tightening in his loins. Unable to resist, he moved to her side and bent to lightly kiss her pink lips.

He walked back to the door and gazed at her one last time, wanting to store the beautiful picture of her in his mind. Then, he grabbed an extra blanket and pillow and headed for the sofa.

When Cassie awoke the next morning, she heard Joshua moving around in the living room. She watched him sit down on the sofa and put his briefcase on the coffee table. He flipped open the attaché and Cassie watched him grimace with pain as he turned his neck. After rotating his head a few times, he groaned and rubbed the side of his neck.

On impulse, she walked into the room and put her hands on his neck, moving her fingers in a soothing motion against the taut muscles. "Nothing like a good night's rest on a sofa that's too short, is there?"

Glancing over his shoulder, he gave her a pained smile. "I'm fine. It's just a little tight this morning."

"It's okay, Joshua." Cassie chuckled as she continued the massage. "You don't have to act all macho on my account."

"You think this is acting macho?" he asked incredulously.

She felt his muscles tighten under her fingers, and before she knew it, he tumbled her over his shoulder until she landed in his lap.

Gripping his shirt tightly, she blinked to ease the vertigo from her sudden spin. When she focused, she saw his devilish smile and was about to ask him where he'd left his mind, when he laughed.

His arms fastened around her like steel bands, and he drew her closer with unmistakable intent. A shiver ran through her at the sound of his deep voice. "Now, this is macho."

And he hungrily devoured her mouth with his own. Joshua had intended this maneuver as shock treatment to get Cassie back for teasing him about his neck. But he hadn't been prepared for the heat that coursed through his veins and brought a pleasurable tightening to his loins.

"Oh, Lord, woman, you're like a drug," he whispered against her lips. "And I'm addicted."

She was soft and relaxed from her sleep and to Joshua she felt supremely feminine, even though she wore his terry robe. Succumbing to the urge to taste her, he ran his tongue along the seam of her lips and captured her gasp with his mouth.

When their mouths separated, their breathing was

labored and Joshua and Cassie looked at each other with dazed expressions.

"Cassie, let me in your life."

She laughed and looked down at where she was sitting. "I kinda think you're already in my life, Joshua."

Intercepting his intent gaze, she sobered. "The million-dollar question is just how in each other's lives we want to get."

Joshua agreed and realized he didn't know the answer to the question either. He just knew that he wanted Cassie for more than a night, for more than a month, for a long time. He'd never lived with a woman before, but found the idea of sharing breakfast with Cassie on a regular basis very appealing. He sensed, however, he might be pushing things to ask her to move into his temporary apartment. "I want more from you than one night. How about let's just take it one day at a time?"

The unreadable expression in his eyes made her feel vaguely uneasy, but she could accept his statement. She certainly couldn't deny her feelings for him anymore. Anyway, they had several things going against them right now, with both of them tied up with their businesses.

"Okay. One day at a time," she said tentatively.

Joshua grinned. Her concession wasn't much, so why did he feel like letting out a rebel yell? Hugging her tightly, he began to plant tiny kisses along her forehead. "Now that we've got that settled," he said enjoying her soft sigh, "let's start the day off right . . . back in my bed."

His kisses started shivers up her spine and she was tempted to follow his suggestion, but she still wasn't totally comfortable with this idea of a relationship with

Joshua. She needed some space. Firmly removing herself from his arms and lap, she stood beside the sofa. "That's a wonderful idea, but I have work to do, and Maggie's coming to the shop today. So, I need to get back to my house to change clothes." A certain vulnerability flashed in his eyes and was gone so quickly she could have imagined it. Still, Cassie felt a tug at her heartstrings at the thought of hurting him after he'd been so caring. She softened the rejection with a kiss on his cheek.

"Come on," she said with a teasing smile. "You're tempting me when I need you to give me a ride home."

"Tempting," Joshua grumbled. He gave her bottom a playful swat and secretly grinned at her exclamation. "The least you can do is show a little mercy and get fully dressed." His mind was busy with plans for the evening as he watched her speedy exit.

One hour later, Cassie groaned and braced herself against the crushing sense of defeat when she surveyed her desecrated shop again. If she allowed, the defeat could swallow her like a tidal wave. But she refused to give in to it, looking forward to that time when she was relocated and flourishing once again. Realizing Maggie would arrive within an hour, she pushed up her sleeves and thrust herself into her task. She became so absorbed in her work that Cassie didn't realize Maggie had walked through the door until she heard the older woman's gasp.

"Oh, my Lord, Cassie," Maggie exclaimed. "I don't think I've ever seen such a mess in my life."

"It's pretty bad," Cassie voiced a concession, then continued with determination. "Joshua's going to send a cleaning crew in here soon. But I wanted to go through and see what we could salvage for when we move. And the insurance company will need an estimate."

She shrugged and gave Maggie a halfhearted attempt at a smile. "Although the agent that came by yesterday said it looked like a total loss to him."

Maggie gazed in bewilderment at Cassie. "Are you still determined to move this shop and get it running somewhere else? I mean, Cassie, as much as I love this store I'd have to think twice about keeping it going at this point." Maggie lifted her arms. "You're gonna have to start from the ground up again, and you don't even have a place to go yet."

Cassie set her chin. Although everything that Maggie had said was true, Cassie was still determined to keep her store. Plenty of people would consider her crazy, but she had to continue. She'd found her niche in this store and she wasn't about to give it up and go work for someone else. Sure, the store had brought her plenty of headaches and tense moments. The building of this business had not made her rich, but it had given her a wealth of confidence and satisfaction. Her voice reflected her resolve. "I'm making a list of everything worth saving so I can contact my suppliers and ask them to send me what I need. I haven't found a place yet, but I'm going out with my realtor tomorrow morning. Something's bound to turn up soon."

She softened her tone. "Listen, Maggie, I know this is a messy job and I'll understand completely if you'd rather not do it. After all, I can pay you for today, but I won't be able to pay you again until I open at the new location. This probably looks like a sinking ship to you, but I can't quit."

When Cassie finished, she saw tears in Maggie's eyes. Cassie gave into the urge and reached out to hug the older woman.

Maggie sniffed loudly. "Now, don't mind me," she protested. "I'm the one who should be comforting you. Cassie, I remember what a blue funk I'd been in after my husband died before I came to work for you. I'm a changed person, and it's all to your credit. I'm with you to the bloody end." Maggie gave her a brief squeeze and Cassie felt herself fighting back her own tears at the older woman's words.

Maggie stepped back and after blowing her nose set her purse down with a loud plop. "I'm here and ready to go. You just tell me what you want me to do."

Cassie explained her system, if one could call it that, of separating the salvageable from the destroyed and packing the salvageable into boxes. The two women made rapid progress, and by the time Maggie left, Cassie estimated they could finish the rest in half a day.

Thankful that she'd worn old jeans today, Cassie stood and stretched. With a moan at her aching muscles, she made herself a promise to soak in the bathtub for not less than an hour tonight. A knock at the door accelerated her pulse at the thought of Joshua. Although he hadn't said he'd be by the store, he assured her that he would see her later. And for the first time in a long time, Cassie looked forward to having a man in her life. There was something just plain wonderful about having someone waiting for her at the end of the day who wanted to see her as much as she wanted to see him. While she felt uncomfortable about the idea of commitment, she'd decided to take a cue from Scarlett O'Hara and think about it tomorrow.

She opened the door and her smile fell into a puzzled frown when she saw Joshua's business partner at the door. A cleaning-service crew waited behind him.

Ken Blomburg smiled at her and pointed past the door. "I got a call from Joshua on my machine. He said the place was a total loss and that he'd be getting a cleaning crew in here soon. So, how about letting us in so I can let these guys get to work?"

Cassie sizzled with anger. She thought she'd already covered this issue with Joshua. Furthermore, her rent was paid through the end of the month. She moved in front of the doorway and shook her head. "I'm sorry you made these arrangements without consulting me first. I'm still sifting through the merchandise to see what's usable."

He shifted impatiently from foot to foot. "Listen, Cassandra, that's your name isn't it?" When she nodded, he continued. "I had to twist some arms to get this cleaning service here today, and I cut some business short so I could drive down from Raleigh. There can't be that much worth keeping. Why don't you just let your insurance cover it and save yourself some work?"

He was trying to maneuver her and she didn't like it one bit. Cassie couldn't help wondering just how much Joshua knew about this, but she pushed the thought aside and said in her firmest voice, "I'm sorry you made these arrangements, but the earliest possible date that I'll be out will be Monday."

"Didn't Joshua talk to you about this? I left him a message on his machine." His exasperation was evident in both his face and tone.

"Joshua mentioned a cleaning service yesterday, but

I told him I wanted to salvage what I could first."
Cassie hesitated briefly when she saw that he made no
move to dismiss the cleaning crew. "Ken, I'm sure I
don't have to remind you that my rent is paid up until
the end of the month and I don't have to be out of the
building until then."

With a heavy sigh, he turned to the cleaning crew
and assured them he would be contacting them soon.
After they left, he turned back to Cassie and asked,
"Well, can I at least see how much this mess will set
us back?" He raised his palms. "I promise. No hidden
Hefty bags."

Cassie chuckled at his earnest expression and moved
away from the door. When Ken walked in, a low whis-
tle escaped his lips and he shook his head. "They really
trashed it, didn't they?" Without waiting for her
response, he continued, "The cleaning crew and a good
paint job will take care of most of it. But the floor's
wrecked, too." He ran the toe of his shoe over a paint
stain on the floor, then looked over at Cassie.

"This must be pretty rough for you, even though you
were going to have to move soon anyway. I was sure
Joshua would be able to get you out of here by now.
He's usually great at negotiating." he narrowed his
eyes at her. "Could be he's a little distracted." He
laughed lightly. "Can't say I blame him. Listen,
Cassandra."

"Cassie," she corrected.

He shrugged. "Cassie. I know you've got your own
business to look out for, but this store's really important
to Joshua. Something about making good in his hometown after his dad was such a bum. I don't know what

your relationship is with him, but I'd hate to see him mess up this store because of you."

Cassie was taken aback and a little offended by his words. "I have no intention of messing up his business. It's not my fault we've been working at cross purposes. The same owner who told you I'd be amenable to leaving assured me that whoever bought this place would let me stay." She crossed her arms defensively over her chest. "And as far as my relationship with Joshua, I don't think that's any of your business."

Ken raised his hand. "Hey, don't get all huffy. I just thought that if you cared about Joshua you ought to know there's more to this than just another store." Ken shrugged and turned to leave. "I'd better be leaving before I get myself into more trouble with my mouth." He grinned sheepishly. "You can see why Joshua's usually the one to handle negotiations. He doesn't have foot-in-the-mouth disease like I do."

Cassie watched him walk to the door and even though he had offended her, she realized Ken meant well and that he was a true friend to Joshua. She found herself liking him despite his blunt nature. "Ken, just for the record, I do care for Joshua. A great deal. I appreciate you sharing what you did with me. It helps me understand him better."

Ken turned and gave her another lopsided grin. "He said you were a peach. Now I can see why."

NINE

Cassie surfaced slowly from her state of semi-consciousness. There was a rapping sound and a man's voice—impatient voice, she corrected herself. Cassie grimaced. The bath water had grown cool and the bubbles had long ago dissolved.

The rapping continued and Cassie blinked owlishly as she identified Joshua's voice.

"Open up this door. Damn it! Cassie, I swear I'll break it down if you don't open up."

Perplexed at the sense of *deja vu*, she rose and shoved her hands through a robe. Ah, the light dawned on her memory. She wasn't going crazy. Joshua had beat on her door and yelled at her when she was sick. Oddly satisfied that she could identify the memory, she strolled to the front door.

Punctuated by loud raps on her door, his voice called to her. She shook her head at his language, wondering what the neighbors would think of her late-night guest.

She calmly swung open the door. "Have a seat, Joshua. I need to finish drying myself." Then she walked back to the bathroom, leaving him staring after her.

She leisurely dried herself and heard him pacing in her living room. Snickering, she donned a hot-pink caftan and tried to figure out what had sent him into this tizzy.

Crossing her arms under her breasts as she re-entered the room, she leaned against the doorway and shrugged at his agitated state. His hands were shoved into his trouser pockets. His tie had been discarded, and his ruffled hair had obviously fallen victim to his raking hand. "Would you like some coffee? Or would some herbal tea help settle your nerves?"

He looked at her tentatively, as if she would turn into an alien at any moment, and Cassie was baffled at his manner.

"Joshua, what is your problem?"

He heaved a great sigh and approached her. "Ken caught up with me and told me about the mix-up with the cleaning crew. He told me you weren't pleased. I figured you might think that I put him up to it." He touched her cheek and spoke earnestly. "I swear I had no idea he was planning this."

"I believe you."

No sooner had the words left her lips then he gathered her into his arms and claimed her mouth with his own. It was a brief but possessive kiss that left her breathless. She took a moment to get her bearings and pulled a little away to look at him quizzically.

"When you didn't answer the door, I guessed that

you were pretty angry, and I panicked. That's why I was yelling and beating at your door."

She sighed and let her head fall against his chest and started to giggle.

"Cassie, what's going on? Are you crying?" Joshua sounded perplexed, then indignant. "You're laughing!"

Unable to contain her mirth, she looked up at him and giggled again. "I'm sorry, Joshua. I'm just trying to figure out how to explain the madman at my door to my neighbors in the morning."

He grinned and swung her up into his arms. "Madman, huh?" She shrieked. "You've hit that right on the mark. You've driven me stark raving mad since the first time I saw you."

He gazed down at her seductively. "So, how are you planning to cure my madness?"

Enjoying this playful side to Joshua, she teased back. "I'm not sure I want to cure it."

He frowned thoughtfully. "Okay, I'm incurable. I can accept that. As long as I'm treatable. What do you say to that?"

Cassie felt the touch of fire from his eyes run through her veins. She asked huskily, "What treatment do you recommend?"

His eyes darkened dramatically and he walked down the hall to her bedroom. He eased her down his hard body with agonizing slowness and cupped her hips against his, leaving her in no doubt as to his state of arousal. Bending forward, he rested his forehead against hers. His voice was low and rough. "The treatment I recommend is you and me on your bed with nothing between us."

Closing her eyes, she felt herself go moist and hot

at his words and touch. She licked her dry lips and stretched against him. His groan excited her even more. "This madness," she breathed against his lips, "seems to be catching. Perhaps we'd better start that treatment now."

He rubbed his mouth against hers and magnified her need when he coaxed her lips open to outline them with his tongue. He swallowed her gasp. As he deepened the kiss, she pulled awkwardly at the buttons on his shirt. The other night she'd spent in Joshua's arms had only whetted her appetite. She craved the beauty and unity that only he could bring her. While her lack of experience had made her tentative before, the hunger she felt for him drove her to boldly express her passion for this man.

Her hunger. His need.

His groans of praise and obvious arousal eliminated her self-consciousness and insecurity. She scattered open-mouthed kisses along his neck and raked her fingers through the whirls of his chest hair. She nipped lightly at his nipples and felt him clench his hands roughly in her hair.

Their harsh breaths filled the silence of her apartment. "I just want to give back some of what you've given me, Joshua." Her aqua eyes pleaded with him. She ran her hand down his taut stomach to his swollen masculinity. "Show me how to please you."

"Oh, God, Cassie," Joshua choked out his response. "You're a dream come true. I look at you and go up in flames." Impatient with her silky caftan, he pulled it up over her head. His heart jumped into his throat at the sight of her, gloriously naked. A vision of creamy glowing skin. Her eyes beckoned him. The quintessential woman. He ran his hand lightly over her hair to her shoulder and breast. This woman could break his heart. The realization hit him with the force of a knock-out punch. Momentarily stunned, his mouth dried and he swallowed hard.

He was in love with her. She moved closer to him and kissed his chest again. Her lips glanced each of his ribs and she bent to her knees and bathed his belly button with her tongue. He ran shaky fingers through her silky hair. His desire to possess her made him grit his teeth in an effort to gain control.

This beautiful woman was adoring him with her mouth and hands because she wanted to give to him. She unbuttoned his slacks and eased the zipper over his bulging manhood. He licked his dry lips as his breath sifted through his mouth. She was operating on instinct alone and driving him completely over the edge. He shuddered at the realization of her power over him.

Spellbound, he watched her push his pants and briefs down his hips. She stopped and looked at him with her heart in her eyes. Then, with her gaze still locked on his, she leaned forward and put her sweet lips on that part of him that ached only for her.

With an anguished cry, he pulled her to his feet and joined his mouth with hers. He engaged her tongue in a wild dance, showing her how much he needed her. Quickly dispensing with the rest of his clothing, he lowered their bodies to the bed and said, "I need to be inside you. I need to feel you around me. But I want you as crazy for me as I am for you."

His hands found her dewy and wanting him. He feasted on her nipples while his fingers drove her higher and higher. Her face was flushed with desire, their bodies were slick. Her fingernails scored his back and she whimpered. "Joshua, please."

"Tell me what you want."

"You," she pleaded breathlessly as his hand threatened to send her into oblivion.

"How?" he asked harshly, his control nearly spent.

"Fill me," she sobbed. "Fill me with only you."

She'd barely uttered her request before he entered her in one long, powerful stroke that sent her into a blinding climax. He held her tightly as she trembled down from the clouds. He lay inside her and murmured his praise into her ear. Her body had just calmed when he began his smooth stroking inside her. She felt the renewed tension within her and her eyes, wide with wonder, locked with Joshua's possessive gaze. Her body joined in the slick rhythm with his.

She'd never felt anything more sensuous in her life than Joshua's consuming gaze on her as he led their bodies and souls to new heights. She watched his face clench in ecstasy as he reached his peak and then she found herself spiraling upward with him.

Their bodies replete, he collapsed on top of her. Yet, instead of feeling uncomfortable under his weight, she savored the sensation of being completely enveloped by him inside and out.

He stirred and groaned. When he started to move away from her, she wrapped her legs more tightly around him.

"Cassie," he protested. "I'll crush you. Let me lie beside you."

"No, I want you to stay where you are." *Forever*, she added silently and wondered where that thought came from.

He raised his head and looked at her intently, correctly interpreting her request. Kissing her forehead in a reassuring manner, he said "If you turn over with me, we can still be together." He gently turned them both and after she had drifted off to sleep he whispered the words he'd held back when he'd loved her with his body.

"I love you."

When Cassie awoke the next morning, she wasn't as shocked with the instant knowledge that Joshua was in her bed. In fact, if pressed, she'd have to say there was something very right about his male presence among her ruffles and lace. But she didn't want to examine the implications of her reasoning. She just wanted to enjoy the sight of this magnificent man who desired her so.

Well, she'd done it now. Cassandra Warner had taken a lover and she didn't regret it one bit. Perhaps, this was what was missing from her life—a mutually satisfying relationship without strings. She winced at that. It sounded cold even to her. Still, she wasn't ready for a long-term commitment, and she was thankful it appeared that Joshua wasn't either. A little voice in the back of her mind disagreed, but she ignored it and leaned over to kiss Joshua's closed eyelids.

She only got close enough for her breath to touch his face before he grabbed her and brought her on top of him. He opened his sexy eyes and drawled, "Like what you see?"

She punched him lightly. "How long have you been awake?"

"Ever since you turned over, and you didn't answer

my question.'' He pulled one of her arms to his lips and kissed the sensitive skin of her inner arm.

"The size of your ego could compete with the Empire State Building, Joshua Daniels.'' She struggled not to shiver from his touch.

He said nothing to that. He just raised an eyebrow in persistent inquiry and began nibbling on her shoulder.

Sighing dramatically, she said, ''Yes, as a matter of fact, I was admiring you . . . that is, until you opened your mouth,'' she finished testily.

He stopped and pulled her face down to his. He rubbed his open mouth a hair's breadth away from her lips and murmured, ''So, you don't like my mouth.''

She strained forward, but he held her that enticing distance away from him, just enough to drive every thought but his mouth from her mind.

''I didn't say that.''

He blew against her ear. ''Hmmm, then what did you say?''

''I was just teasing,'' she protested, growing frustrated with his elusive movements. She wanted him to kiss her now.

She felt the rumble of a deep chuckle from his chest. ''That's all I'm doing,'' he said mildly. ''Just teasing.''

She groaned and kissed the cleft in his chin. ''Torturing,'' she corrected.

He cocked his head and looked at her. ''Torture's not so bad, Cassie, depending on the kind.'' His eyes issued a lascivious invitation she couldn't refuse.

She reached down to dip her tongue into the cleft she had just kissed, inflicting her own brand of torture in the process. She delighted in the tightening of his body in response to her. "Perhaps a demonstration is in order."

And Joshua captured her mouth with his own as he led her on a wicked journey that lent new meaning to the concept of agony and ecstasy.

Much later, she pushed her hair from her face and grimaced at the time displayed on her clock radio.

"I've got to go, Joshua." She reached over to throw the covers off of her when he clasped her arm. When she glanced over her shoulder at him, she glimpsed a fleeting expression of hurt and bewilderment.

"Go where? It's Saturday."

"I've an appointment with my realtor in," she glanced at the clock again, "twenty-nine minutes."

She watched the wheels turn in his mind at her response.

He whipped the covers off of both of them. "I'll go with you."

Feeling odd about his presence on her scouting trip when he was partially responsible, she hesitated.

"Joshua, I don't know if that's a good idea. It's going to be both grueling and boring for you. I asked the realtor to pack in as much as possible because of my limited time." Furthermore, she had a feeling he might not approve of her prospective locations and she'd already faced the fact that she was going to have to compromise some of her requirements in order to get a lower rent.

He looked disappointed. "Don't you want me to go?"

"It's not that." She hated seeing him so disappointed. She turned the table and put him on the spot. "Why would you want to go?"

"To be with you," he answered promptly. "And to lend an expert opinion. I've scouted the locations for all our fast-print stores thus far." He shrugged. "Of course, if you're still bearing a grudge, then I can see why you wouldn't want me to go."

He'd boxed her in with that statement. If she admitted to feeling uneasy about his presence because he'd bought her building, she'd appear petty. "Okay." She glanced at the clock one last time and warned him, "But you've got to be ready to leave in twenty-three minutes and I get dibs on the shower."

She quickly scooted off the bed and dashed to the bathroom as he called after her, "Why don't we save time and take it together."

Laughing, she retorted, "I don't need the distraction."

Eight hours later, Cassie and Joshua dragged their tired bodies back into her apartment and collapsed on the sofa. Groaning, she covered her face with her hands and relived her location scouting trip.

It had been a nightmare.

Joshua had found something wrong with every place they visited. Granted, his comments had been truthful, but his criticisms had run her realtor straight up the wall. Cassie wouldn't have been surprised if the poor woman didn't burn her realtor certification papers and enter a different occupation. She hadn't encouraged Cassie to call her back.

At the last store, Cassie had finally asked Joshua to put a lid on it, and now he was mad at her. She slit her eyes over at his profile. His arms were crossed over his chest in defiance. His jaw was clenched and she expected his lower lip to jut out any minute in a recalcitrant pout.

All at once, the situation struck her as terribly amusing and she gave a little chuckle. When he turned to glare at her accusingly, she tried to stifle it, but that only made it worse and she laughed again.

Although she could see he was trying to remain serious, his lips began to twitch and he said, "Mind sharing the joke."

"This had to be one of the biggest disasters I've ever had the opportunity to be a part of." She wiped the tears of mirth from her eyes. "I mean, I've had cakes fall and dinners that burned, but this . . ."

He grinned. "It was pretty bad, wasn't it? Did you see your realtor's face when I told her that the only way they'd get somebody to move into that third building was if the owners paid the renters."

"Mm, hmm, I thought I'd die when you started talking about realtor's commissions being one of the biggest problems for entrepreneurs." Cassie shook her head and scolded him gently. "You were pretty hard on her, considering all the trouble she went to."

"Hey," he defended himself, "she should have done a more thorough job. There were major flaws with every single one of the properties she showed you."

Sighing, she countered, "Yes, but you seem to forget that money is a major issue with me. I'd love to find a location downtown, but I can't afford the payments. I'm going to have to compromise. I'm going to try to set up another appointment with her for Tuesday."

Joshua's brows furrowed. "Are you sure you want to do it on Tuesday? I have a full day. Why don't you—"

Gently, but firmly she interrupted. "You're not invited."

She saw the frustration cross his face and moved closer to him. "Joshua, I've got to face facts, and I've got to move fast."

He sighed thoughtfully. "I can accept that. But if you don't have anything planned for tomorrow, could you come with me to my mother's for lunch?" He grinned ruefully. "She's been hounding me to bring you since she met you."

Cassie shifted uneasily. Lunch with mother sounded serious, sounded like commitment, and Cassie wasn't ready for commitment. She'd just gotten over accepting her attraction to Joshua. The fact that she cared deeply for him shook her to the extent that she didn't want to admit it even to herself.

Joshua read Cassie's face like a book. The expression on her face bespoke discomfort and apprehension. Although he strained at the bit to push their relationship along, he contained himself, barely, and opted for giving her some space. She reminded him of a skittish prize filly dancing close and then moving out of his reach. Still, he'd made headway; she'd accepted him into her bed and into her life. He knew she cared about him, even if she wouldn't speak the words. She would be his, if only he could be patient.

"Now that I think of it, you're probably going to be busy with your inventory." He smiled reassuringly. "We can just take a rain check."

Cassie sighed in relief. "Thanks, uh, I appreciate your coming along today, Joshua, but I'm really beat. With everything that's happening with my store, and last night . . .'' Her voice trailed off and her cheeks turned pink.

She began again, "What I mean to say is, I—"

Joshua broke in with a lazy smile. "You're not trying to get rid of me, are you?" He eliminated the distance separating their bodies by pulling her next to him.

His nearness jolted her pulse and she protested. "No, I've just got a lot to do, and . . ." Her voice trailed off again as he nuzzled her ear and lightly kissed her jaw.

"You were saying?" he prompted as he kissed her eyelids.

A soft sigh escaped her lips.

"You were saying something about having a lot to do." He kissed the corner of her lips.

She groaned and pushed him away. "Yes, I have a lot to do," she said defensively. "I haven't slept well since before the vandalism, and I can't sleep with you."

"Why not?"

Standing upright in an attempt to shake off the spell he cast over her, she crossed her arms under her breasts and decided to appease his colossal ego. "Because I find I don't want to sleep when I'm with you." Cassie walked to her door and opened it.

Joshua stood reluctantly. "There's no way I can persuade you to let me to stay?"

"I didn't say that," she insisted. "But I'm counting on you to be an honorable man and let me get some things done."

He saw that she was serious and there was a tinge of desperation in her voice. Walking to her, he dropped a tender kiss on her lips. "I'll see you tomorrow." He touched her chin. "When you're getting your beauty sleep, dream of me."

Cassie watched his long, masculine stride as he walked to his car, and after three hours of concentrated work on her store inventory list, she fell into bed and did exactly as he suggested. She dreamed of Joshua.

Over the next days, they developed a pattern; their days were spent apart from each other and their nights were spent together. Cassie finished clearing out the salvageable merchandise of her shop on Monday, and with a last tearful look over what had once been her pride and joy, she bade the shop good-bye.

After another frustrating trip with her realtor on Tuesday, she felt her first real taste of defeat and was in no mood to hear of how smoothly Joshua's plans for his store were going. She'd just about decided to call him up and cancel their plans for pizza and a rented movie when her phone rang.

Her brother Ben had heard about the vandalism through her mom and he pumped her for details on her plans.

"So, whatcha gonna do now, Cass?"

Cassie sighed. This wasn't the best time to be asking that question. "I'm shaking the bushes for another location, but so far the bushes have come up empty."

"Hmm, you sound a little discouraged."

She filled him in on her two fruitless and frustrating searches for a new location, and he murmured sympathetically. But, before she knew it, he'd turned the conversation around to Joshua and grilled her on their progress. She stubbornly refused to comment until he started humming the wedding march.

"Cut it out, Ben!" she huffed, not hearing Joshua slip in the door. "We're just friends. It's only a platonic relationship. Besides," she further stated her case, "if I were going to marry someone, and I'm not planning on it for the next hundred years, I wouldn't pick someone like Joshua Daniels. He doesn't exactly strike me as the faithfully-committed type." She snapped her mouth shut, uneasily aware that she'd exposed one of her deepest fears. Then, before Ben could comment, she changed the subject.

"You know, brother dear, if it was your intention to cheer me up with this discussion, I think you should know you've failed miserably."

Ben laughed. "Hey, you gotta admit a little healthy anger is a lot better than a boat load of heavy depression. But, I'll back off. Chin up, kid. Remember, you've got the Warner stubbornness. I'll call you later."

Later to Ben could mean next week or next month, Cassie thought, as she hung up the phone. Groaning, she turned around and gave a little start when she saw Joshua.

His eyes glinted. His usually tempting mouth was set in a grim line, and his stance was that of an offended bull. He was angry.

Cassie winced when she remembered how she had described Joshua and their relationship. She wondered how she was going to smooth this over.

Quirking an eyebrow, he said coolly, "Platonic? Just friends?"

When she didn't immediately respond, he clipped out his last question. "Answer me this, Cassie, just how many men have you had this kind of platonic, just friends relationship with?'' he finished mockingly.

She hadn't wanted to hurt his feelings, but something about his tone set her on edge. Who did he think he was to question her about her previous love life, meager though it might be? He hadn't exactly provided her with a resume on his past love life. Sure, he'd told her that he'd always taken responsibility in his past affairs, but he hadn't revealed how many there'd been. And, although she hated the feeling of vulnerability, she wondered if she were one in a long line of women.

She held her temper in check and answered just as coolly. ''That's none of your business. But before you get irrational, you might want to know that Ben has always considered my love life a source of amusement. The only time he's been the least bit sympathetic toward me was when my engagement was cancelled. His recommendation was for him and Ross to terminate the future of Billy Joe's reproductive activities.'' Cassie rolled her eyes. ''I realize that was a misguided attempt to protect me, and I love him for it, but I don't want Ben to know about our relationship.''

''Is it because you're ashamed?''

''No!'' she said in astonishment. ''I don't want Ben's advice. I don't want his cute little jokes. I don't want his interference.''

Joshua felt tentatively relieved. She didn't seem ashamed. But it had hurt him tremendously to hear her describe their relationship as platonic when he was growing more deeply in love with her with each passing day. She appeared nervous and earnest. Joshua reasoned that she must care more than she was admitting.

''Okay, I'll buy that, but I think I deserve to know

if this is your normal practice; telling your brother that your lover is just a friend."

She shifted uneasily from foot to foot, reluctant to reveal the truth of her inexperience, but also knowing that he wasn't going to be satisfied until she answered him. She compromised with her uneasiness and his persistence by hedging. "I think you've observed that I don't exactly have a vast amount of experience. Certainly," she said pointedly, "not as much as you do."

Now it was Joshua's turn to squirm. How could he explain the difference between his past relationships with women and his dreams of a future with Cassie? He couldn't, so he danced around the issue just as she had. "I'm not a monk. I've already told you that I've had other relationships, but I've acted responsibly." *You don't need to worry about those other women*, he continued silently, *I love you.*

She hadn't been talking about contraception, and she'd bet he knew that, too. His hedging left her uncomfortable, but there was something in his eyes she couldn't read. Something tender and honest. It cooled her anger and warmed her heart at the same time.

"We're not getting anywhere with this discussion." She gave a little coaxing smile. "If you're not still angry with me and I'm not still angry with you, then we could probably discuss something more important like what kind of pizza we should have tonight."

The woman was a killer. He'd been ready to walk out when he'd overheard the phone conversation with her brother, and now she had him eating out of her hand. Joshua surrendered, but with a reminder of just how un-platonic their relationship truly was, he pulled her to him and planted a hard, possessive kiss on her lips. Her taste tempted him and he deepened the caress, tasting and teasing her tongue into action. The sensuous sliding and thrusting reflected a deeper intimacy. And the result was so carnal that Cassie wore a dazed expression when he dragged his mouth from hers.

He watched her blink and grinned devilishly. "I'll take anything but anchovies."

With her body still crying for the fulfillment of that kiss, Cassie stared at him and wondered what he was talking about.

TEN

After another morning spent trailing her realtor through inappropriate locations for her shop, Cassie began to feel more than a tad desperate. Perhaps she should visit some of the places again, just to make sure she couldn't make do with one of them. Waving good-bye to her realtor, Cassie drove downtown, relieved to be meeting Kim for lunch. She always cheered Cassie up.

A saucy grin lit Kim's face as she met her at a favorite tearoom near the bank where Kim worked. The two women were seated and placed their order.

Kim slit her eyes devilishly. "Cassie, you could make the front page of the *National Enquirer* with everything that's happened to you lately. Tell me if I forget something. First, your former fiance shows up and Joshua knocks the guy senseless, then your store gets vandalized, and when everyone tries to get in touch with you, they find you're spending your nights with

Joshua Daniels. You haven't had the least bit of gossip spread about you up to this point. I tell you, girl, when you do it, you do it right.''

Cassie grimaced at her friend's suggestive tone. ''As a matter-of-fact, you did leave out one tiny detail; something about my very best friends arranging to meet me at a pool and standing me up.'' She paused meaningfully. ''Anything come to mind, Kim?''

Kim had the grace to look chagrined. ''I wondered how mad you'd be. But, Cassie, someone had to do something. It was obvious to everyone except you how right Joshua would be for you. And you know how Fred hates it when I meddle.'' Kim shrugged. ''He went along with my plan without a single protest because Joshua was acting like a wounded bear.

''Besides,'' she glanced speculatively at Cassie, ''considering the amount of time you've spent together lately, I wouldn't think you'd be complaining too much.''

Kim waited while the waiter placed their iced tea on the table. ''So, what's between you two?''

Cassie squirmed uncomfortably. This conversation wasn't going the way she'd planned. Sure, she'd expected a little good-natured teasing from her best friend. She hadn't expected to be grilled. Tempted to offer Kim the same explanation she'd given her brother, Cassie looked to each side of herself and thought better of it. Knowing her luck, if Joshua wasn't within hearing distance, he'd hear second- or third-hand what she'd said about him. Somehow, deceiving Kim felt like a betrayal to Joshua, and she found she couldn't do that to him.

Her lovelife hadn't been up for discussion in a long

time, but she could deny the truth only so long to her friends. "Joshua and I are seeing each other," she began tentatively. "He's been very good to me, and . . . he's special to me."

Cassie breathed a sigh of relief. There, that wasn't so bad, she thought with a smile. Joshua would even approve.

The waiter brought their hot, thinly sliced roast beef sandwiches and the women dug in appreciatively.

"Any chance we'll be hearing wedding bells soon?"

Cassie's throat closed and she choked on the bite of sandwich. She washed it down with some tea, and stammered her response, "No! We haven't known each other long enough." She stared at her friend in exasperation. "Kim, could we possibly discuss something else?"

"Oh, I get it," Kim said in understanding, "Cassie's shy." When Cassie started to protest, Kim shook her head and continued, "That's okay, I won't razz you anymore. I'm just glad you're hooked up with someone like Joshua. I will warn you, though," she said between bites, "Fred says Joshua has it bad for you, so I wouldn't be surprised if he isn't planning something long-range."

She waved her hand. "Enough of that. What's going on with your store?"

And though Cassie filled her friend in on the latest developments, she wondered about Kim's warning. She wondered about the feeling of both excitement and dread at the thought of a long-term relationship with Joshua. But she pushed it aside with the realization that he seemed perfectly content with their relationship as it stood; no strings, one day at a time.

With a promise to get together again soon, Kim and Cassie went their separate ways. Cassie headed back to her apartment and was pretty glum by the time Joshua walked through her door that evening. She had balanced her checkbook and worked out her budget a dozen different ways. She concluded, with a sick feeling in the pit of her stomach, that unless she found a location for her store very soon, she was going to be out on the street looking for a job.

He strode into the living room with a wide grin on his face. Grumpily, she envied his good mood. She was tempted to tell him to take his good mood somewhere else before he reached for her and swept her into his arms, swinging her around and around. His hard kiss on her lips made a smacking sound, and his eyes seemed to glow.

Delighted in spite of herself, she asked, "Which sweepstakes did you win today?"

"None," he said. "Unless you count the Cassie Warner sweepstakes. I get a lifetime supply of kisses." He chuckled at her uncomprehending expression and rocked her in his arms.

"I have a surprise for you."

"What?" She pretended to give the matter serious thought. "Godiva chocolates?"

He shook his head. "Better."

"Hmmm, Rocky Road ice cream."

He shook his head again. "Better."

"Okay." She lifted her palms in surrender. She couldn't help but smile in the face of such boundless enthusiasm. He looked like he was ready to explode. "You've got me. What is it?"

"I'm not going to tell you what it is. I'm going to show you. Come on, woman, get your shoes on."

Curiosity emanating from her every pore, she coaxed, "Couldn't you give me just one hint?"

"No," he said adamantly. "Get your shoes."

"Do I need to dress up?" she called from the bedroom as she slipped on her shoes and took a quick peek in the mirror. She straightened her pink cotton sweater and smoothed her pants.

"No," he said with a hint of impatience. "And you need to hurry up, because we need to get there before dark."

"My, my," she teased, watching him jingle the keys in his pocket. "I don't believe I've ever seen you in this much of a rush." She grabbed her pocketbook and joined him at the door. She was dying of curiosity, and he wasn't giving her one hint. Hoping this surprise didn't involve a visit to his mother or anything of that nature, she asked uncertainly, "Are you sure I'm going to like this?"

"No."

He smiled at her glare. "You're gonna love it."

Cassie knitted her brows as they drove downtown. She'd pestered him so during the first part of the ride that he'd told her he wasn't answering anymore questions until they reached their destination. When he slowed down at her shop's previous location, she looked over at him completely baffled. "Joshua, I'm sure you're making great headway renovating the store, but I can't believe the contractors have made it unrecognizable already."

"We're not going to my building," he said as he

pulled into a parking space directly in front of his building.

Cassie looked around, noting that all of the other businesses were closing for the evening. "But, everything else is closed."

He got out of his car in a smooth stride and opened her door. Holding a key in front of her nose, he corrected, "Not everything."

Joshua was milking this for all it was worth. It was so rare that he had an opportunity to pull one over on Cassie. Chuckling lightly, he pressed the key into her palm and led her to the door of the vandalized dress shop. "It's all yours if you want it."

Cassie appeared totally confused. "But, this is Mrs. Freeman's dress shop. I've known her for years. I thought she was just going to close up for the summer because of the damage to her inventory."

Joshua shook his head. "She's closing up for good. She took what she could get from the insurance company and chose to retire." He paused and gestured at the door where she still stood. "Go ahead, what are you waiting for?"

Cassie shook her head as if this was too much for her to comprehend and unlocked the door. They entered the shop and found it clean and bare. Black paint was still splattered everywhere. "It's smaller than your place, but . . ." She looked around the room, mentally placing her merchandise.

"How much is the rent?"

Joshua named a reasonable figure and she looked at him in astonishment.

She crossed her arms over her chest as if she were

trying to keep from getting too excited, as if the bottom might fall out any minute. "What about the lease?"

"It's negotiable. The owners live out of town so they prefer you warn them far in advance if you want to terminate the contract." He frowned thoughtfully. "The only bad part is that you'll have to cover all that black paint yourself. I tried to get the owners to cover the cost of the paint, but they said either you paint or the rent would have to be raised. I figured you'd rather have a lower rent." He strolled around the room knocking on the walls. "And any structural changes you make will have to be approved, aside from getting rid of the dressing rooms."

He looked back to her then and grinned. "I'm a pretty fair painter, and I'll be glad to lend some muscle if you want those dressing rooms knocked out."

Momentarily speechless, Cassie gaped at him. This was the answer to her problems. She barely knew what to say. "You arranged all of this?"

He looked at her uneasily, unsure if she thought him heavy handed. "I didn't obligate you," he reassured her. "But I did leave a deposit. Cassie," he explained, "you know how quickly these places get snapped up. Your phone was busy when I called, so I had to make a decision to jump on it, or wait."

"How did you find out about this? Wait, let me guess, while I was wearing out my shoes and patience looking at inappropriate properties, you either made one phone call or opportunity walked through the door."

"Well," he walked to her and took her into his arms, "opportunity didn't walk through the door, but the realtor responsible for this shop did. When I told her you might be interested, she was ecstatic that she wouldn't have to list it." He paused. "You're not saying anything. Do you feel like I overstepped?"

Cassie looked at him in disbelief. "You've got to be kidding." When she saw that he wasn't, she reassured him. "I just can't believe it. I spent the entire afternoon working out how long I'd be able to go without getting another job and I was so discouraged before you came home." Smiling, she remembered how easily he had lifted her spirits.

She shrugged, looking around the shop. "You've just given me the world on a platter. I can't begin to imagine how I can repay you."

But Joshua could. He wanted Cassie as his wife. Of course, he wouldn't use his finding a location for her shop as a means of extracting that promise from her. But somewhere along the line, he'd discovered that he wanted her in his life permanently. The thought had thrown him at first because he'd given up on finding the closeness he felt with Cassie. It was more than sex, though he couldn't complain about what they shared in that area. Cassie wanted him for who he was; in spite of his father, in spite of the fact that he hadn't made a verbal commitment to her, and in spite of her own insecurities. Although she hadn't voiced her feelings, she'd told him that she loved him in a thousand ways. With the barrier of the store removed, Joshua believed it should be smooth sailing to get her to agree to be his wife. He'd give her a couple more weeks to get used to having him around, take him to see his mother, and pop the question.

He tightened his hold on her and waggled his eyebrows suggestively. "Are you sure you can't . . . imagine how to thank me?"

She laughed and playfully hit his arm. "Hey, you didn't have to get me a place to put my shop for that." She cocked her head to the side thoughtfully. "Wouldn't you rather have Godiva chocolates?"

"Nope."

She loved the gleam in his dark eyes and pushed a strand from his forehead. "How about a pizza without anchovies?"

"Nope."

His head lowered toward hers and she giggled. "Wait, I've got it." He paused and she whispered in his ear, "Raspberry sherbet."

In turn, he whispered his suggestion for their plans in her ear.

Scandalized, yet aroused, she exclaimed, "Joshua!"

"You don't like my idea?" he asked, his lips pressed against her neck.

His lips elicited a lovely vibrating sensation against her skin and she helplessly arched her neck to give him more room. "I didn't say that," she protested.

He pressed his pelvis against her, revealing his readiness. He gave her a long, wet kiss. Breaking apart, they stared at each other with hazy eyes. He pulled her toward the door. "Let's get out of here. We'll call the realtor later."

After they celebrated in bed, Cassie called the realtor and arranged to sign the lease the following morning. Then, they celebrated again in bed, this time with a pizza without anchovies and soft drinks.

The following days were pure bliss for Cassie. She worked like a Trojan to get her shop ready and spent the evenings with Joshua. She didn't, however, forget that Joshua had been responsible for finding her new location and thanked him endlessly. First, she had a pizza delivered to his store. That ended up doubly nice because he insisted on sharing it with her. Next, she gave him a box of Godiva chocolates. He tried to get her to share those also, but she insisted, with a remarkable amount of fortitude, that he eat every last piece. He'd given her a key to his apartment, so during one of his visits to Raleigh, she left a carton of raspberry sherbet in his freezer.

His deep voice rolled over her like a warm bath when she woke to answer the phone late that same evening. "There's been an elf in my kitchen."

Cassie chuckled huskily. "Oh, really." She yawned. "What makes you say that?"

"Something's in my freezer."

"An elf's in your freezer?"

His laugh brought goose bumps to her flesh. "Are you gonna play dumb?"

"Who, me?" she asked innocently.

Joshua gave a noisy, long-suffering sigh. "Thanks for the sherbet, Cassie. It made me think of you."

She was just starting to wake up. "I remind you of sherbet. Hmmm. I'll have to think on that one."

"Cassie," Joshua paused. "I love sherbet. See ya tomorrow."

Fully awake now, Cassie sat up and replaced the telephone receiver. She stared at the phone, whispering to herself. "Did he say what I think he said?" She replayed the conversation in her head, alternately grasping the significance of his words and dismissing the notion that he loved her.

Still, a thrill ran through her at the thought that Joshua Daniels had said he loved her. Yet, he had only actually said that he loved sherbet, she cautioned herself. And she would go stark raving mad if she didn't stop thinking about it. Cassie dragged herself from bed and drank a glass of warm milk and went back to bed to lay awake thinking of Joshua.

They grew closer emotionally as they shared more time with each other. Cassie had been moved to tears when Joshua told her stories from his early childhood; before he was adopted, he'd been terribly neglected. Joshua confessed that when his biological father had shown up after ten years of absence, he hadn't recognized the man. Yet, he'd always felt an obligation to get him off the street, albeit temporarily. He'd even gone so far as to read some literature on alcoholics, hoping there was something he could do to help cure his father. Joshua reached the conclusion that he didn't want to enable the older man to continue with the disease, so he never gave him any money to buy liquor. A room and breakfast that his father probably never ate were all he provided, along with encouragement to seek medical treatment. Cassie's heart broke for the little boy whose life had been torn apart so needlessly.

A few nights later, after Cassie went to sleep on his shoulder, he relived some of the experiences of his youth. The little boy had grown into a confused and angry teenager, who'd had to contend with malicious gossip even in his adoptive father's church.

"Bad seed," that's what he'd overheard one day when he sought his father after a baseball game. His father rarely raised his voice, but he set the spiteful woman on her way for the insulting advice she'd offered. "Send him back, there's no hope for a bad seed." Although he was pleased his father had defended him, Joshua had always sensed that he looked at him in a different light from that moment on. And the words were ingrained on his psyche.

Perhaps that was why he'd put so much energy into making a success of his business and so little into personal relationships. His entrepreneurial efforts yielded concrete, quantifiable results. The results of personal relationships were much more difficult to define. And although women had often pursued him, he'd felt somehow inadequate at the prospect of a long-term relationship. So, he'd taken his pleasure when he could and built the business.

Joshua looked down at the lovely woman sleeping so trustingly in his arms. How long, he wondered, until she truly belonged to him. While his adoptive parents had done their best, he'd always had this vague sense of not belonging to anyone. And for the first time in his life, he found that more than anything he wanted to belong to Cassie.

She'd granted him space in her life, but now he was ready for more. He brushed a kiss on her sleep-tousled hair and held her tightly, willing her to bind herself to him permanently.

The next morning was Saturday. Joshua slipped out to bring some chocolate croissants and fresh gourmet coffee back for breakfast in bed. Cassie stirred drowsily as he nuzzled her awake. He tickled her nose with a strand of her hair and laughed when she swatted at his hand.

His deep laugh penetrated her slumber and she opened one eye, then turned her face into the pillow.

"Hey, sleepyhead, wake up, I've got fresh coffee and croissants."

She turned her head quickly and sniffed appreciatively. "Croissants?"

Sitting up, she slipped into a robe and rubbed her hands together and licked her lips. "Let me at them."

Joshua chuckled and handed her a cup of coffee. "So, when did your appetite kick in?"

"When you said croissants." She took a sip of the hot liquid. "Thank you. You're a man after my own heart."

"Among other things," he leered playfully.

As they fought over the last crumbs of the pastries, Joshua eased into the subject on his mind. "Since your grand opening is next weekend, how about us driving up to Chapel Hill today? I know this great restaurant where we could have dinner."

"Sounds nice."

Joshua took a deep breath and added mildly, "Plus, I've been invited to the wedding of one of my more important clients."

Cassie's throat closed at the mention of the word wedding, making her wish she hadn't won the battle over that last crumb of croissant. The silence stretched between them, and she realized that Joshua was waiting for her response. She had no idea what to say. Her voice cracked. "This wedding is today?"

"This afternoon."

"Uh, huh." Her mind raced furiously. How could she get out of this?

"Great!" Joshua said with enthusiasm. Standing up, he clasped his palms together with a clapping sound and proceeded to announce his plans. "First, we'll—"

"No!" Cassie cried then lowered her voice. "No, I wasn't saying I'd go," she corrected.

"Oh," Joshua said studying her intently. "Then what were you saying?"

Squirming under his scrutiny, Cassie searched her brain for a plausible response. She smiled apologetically, "I don't have anything to wear." She shrugged. "You see, I haven't taken any of my good dresses to the dry cleaners lately because I've been so busy with the shop."

Her hopes that he would accept her flimsy excuse without further questioning were dashed when he opened her closet door and surveyed the contents. He pulled out a white silk suit that looked as fresh as a daisy and raised his eyebrows. "What's wrong with this?"

"Uh, it might be kind of hot for an outdoor wedding." Cassie prayed this was an outdoor wedding.

To no avail.

"Did I say it was outdoors?" He shook his head. "It's in a nice air-conditioned cathedral." He searched further through the closet and pulled out a pale blue shell. "Will this go with it?"

"Yeees, but—"

"Fine," he interrupted. He glanced at his wristwatch. "We ought to leave by eleven, so—"

"I don't want to go."

He broke off and stared at her. "Why not?"

Cassie looked down at her fingers lacing them and unlacing them as she sighed.

Joshua hung the clothes back in the closet and came to sit beside her on the bed. He took her restless hands in his. "Cassie, this doesn't have anything to do with which dress to wear, does it?"

She continued to stare down at their hands and shook her head from side to side.

His voice was tinged with exasperation. "Well, then, what's the problem? It's not like it's your own wedding."

Cassie jerked her head up, and cleared her throat. "I have this . . . thing about weddings." She stood and pulled her robe around her more securely in a protective motion. "I get sick to my stomach and break out in cold sweat. I don't go to weddings unless I absolutely have to."

"What about Anne's?"

"Anne was my roommate in college, and she asked me to be her bridesmaid." Cassie explained further. "It would have broken her heart if I hadn't come. These people that you're talking about don't know me from Adam."

"But I know them, and I want you to come," Joshua insisted. "You've got to get past this irrational fear about weddings, Cassie. And it might as well be now."

Staring at him in astonishment, she said, "Irrational! You try walking through a decorated church before your wedding day to tell the minister the whole thing is off. Eerie doesn't describe it." She turned accusingly. "And who made you the psychological expert? For that matter, why are you pushing me? You're the one who said to take this one day at a time. I'd think you'd run a country mile from this kind of situation. Us together at a wedding."

Joshua could see this wasn't the best time for this discussion, but the combination of her accusations and his frustration drove him on. "I didn't say I was a psychological expert." He spoke in a chiding tone that came out sounding condescending. "I just think that a mature adult wouldn't want to hang onto this silly aversion."

"Now, I'm silly." Cassie crossed her arms over her chest, her face and voice livid. "Tell you what, Joshua, you go to this wedding. And I don't care how you go, by yourself," she said rashly, "or with someone else. But, I'm not going." She turned to go. "I'm taking a shower and going to my shop."

"That's right, Cassie," Joshua jeered. "Hide in your store like you always do."

She whipped around and glared at him, spitting out her response, "At least my store doesn't want more from me than I can give."

Joshua literally ground his teeth at her response as he watched her race to the bathroom. He winced at the sound of the door slamming, tempted to go break it down and reason with her. More discouraged than ever, he was already remorseful that he'd pushed her so far. He raked his fingers through his hair and paced back and forth.

Fear. He hated the taste of it, the smell of it. Mostly, he hated the feeling. And that's what he was feeling now. He was going to lose her. The dread seeped into his gut. He might be able to patch things up now, but he was going to lose her. For God's sake, the woman couldn't even attend a wedding with him. And no matter how he tried, the fear reminded him of the rejection he'd felt when his natural father would leave him for days when he was a little boy; the mortification he'd felt when the kids at school had made fun of his father.

Uncertain of what to do next, he strode out of the

house to give her some space and to plan his next action.

After they both spent a night in agony, Joshua bought a flower arrangement and delivered it to Cassie along with his stilted apology. Cassie delivered her own stilted apology, and they spent the rest of the day together.

But things changed between them. Where they had once freely shared their thoughts and feelings with each other, now, they approached each other with caution as if they were walking on eggs. Where their lovemaking had grown both tender and passionate, it now seemed tinged with desperation as if they were both grasping tightly to something slipping through their fingers.

Their desperation revealed itself in different ways. As Cassie grew more cheerful, determined to avoid any unpleasantness, Joshua grew more morose. Emotionally, he seemed to retreat, and though Cassie racked her brain for ways to bring him back, nothing worked.

The days turned into weeks, and they both took turns standing by each other's sides at the grand openings of their respective businesses. Cassie watched Joshua change before her eyes. He grew more brooding with each passing day, and though she knew they couldn't continue this way, she couldn't make herself end it. Because, she found to her dismay, a brooding, moody Joshua was better than no Joshua at all.

Amazingly enough, it all came to a head over a little phone call. Joshua was working late, as he had been prone to do lately, and Cassie answered her ringing phone, expecting to hear his voice.

"Oh, Cassie, dear, is that you?" a woman's voice asked.

"Yes."

"This is Mrs. Daniels, Joshua's mother. He gave me your number a few weeks ago in case I couldn't get in touch with him. I don't suppose he's there, is he?"

"Uh, no," Cassie was so stunned that he'd given her number to his mother that she barely knew how to answer. What else had he told her? "Have you checked at work?"

"Yes," Mrs. Daniels sighed. "But that silly answering machine was all I got."

Cassie smiled at the older woman's impatience. "Well, I could have him call you back when, uh, if he comes here." Awkwardly, Cassie continued. "Is this an emergency?"

"Oh, no, darling," she reassured. "I just haven't talked to him in over a week and I wanted to see how he's doing. The last time I saw him, he had these awful black circles under his eyes and he seemed rather distracted." She paused. "You wouldn't know why, would you?"

"Uh, not really." Cassie winced at the fib. If Joshua's mother could see Cassie, she'd get a look at the matching circles under her own eyes. "But, he's been very busy at work lately."

"Yes, but I'm counting on you to change all that. Joshua's told me all about you and how he's planning on making this relationship permanent." She continued in a confiding tone. "Come on, you can tell me. When do y'all plan to announce your engagement?"

"Engagement?" Cassie repeated weakly, stunned

that Joshua had discussed their relationship with his mother.

"Of course." She hesitated then sounded scandalized. "You're not planning to elope, are you?"

"No!" Cassie answered hastily. She had to get off this phone before this woman had her bridesmaid's dresses selected and her children named. "Listen, I have a pot boiling over. I'll have Joshua call you when I see him. Good-bye, Mrs. Daniels."

An odd mix of dread and sadness settled over her after she hung up the phone. She felt ripped in half. Her inability to make a commitment to Joshua was hurting him, leaving him dissatisfied. Try as she might, she couldn't avoid that fact anymore. Their temporary utopia of taking it one day at a time was no more.

Cassie walked into the living room and sank down on the sofa. She didn't even bother turning on the lamp, preferring the cover of darkness over her emotions. How did she feel? Confused. Betrayed. Most of all, sad. Because she'd wanted their relationship to bring as much happiness to Joshua as it had to her, and apparently, it hadn't.

So, what now? If she was so sure a commitment between them wouldn't work, why did she feel sliced up inside at the thought of ending it? She dropped her head into her hands and moaned.

ELEVEN

Joshua found her sitting in the darkness. His eyes adjusted to the dim illumination of moonlight. "Cassie, why are you sitting here in the dark?"

Unobtrusively, Cassie swiped at the dampness that seeped from her eyelids and murmured lowly, "Just thinking."

"About what?" He sat beside her, and a note of concern crept into his voice. "Did something happen at the store?"

"No, no." Again she answered in that low voice.

He watched her exhale slowly, almost painfully.

"Joshua, your mother called tonight."

"Is there an emergency?"

"No, she just wanted to know how you were doing," she answered, and took another slow breath. "But we talked a little bit, and I must say I was surprised at some of the things she told me."

Dread seeped into his being at the tone of her voice.

Dread and relief. He surmised from her expression that his mother had questioned Cassie about her relationship with him, and with Cassie's aversion to commitment, she'd probably been scared witless. At least, they could get it out in the open and he could stop pretending. He could see this was painful for her, so he took the initiative knowing this could well be the end for their relationship.

Taking her hand in his, he said with a rueful smile, "I can just imagine what kinds of things my mother said to you. I think she's been trying to marry me off since I was eighteen." He tried to chuckle lightly, but it didn't quite come off.

Emotion clogged his throat, but he forced himself to continue. "She probably asked you if we'd set a wedding date or something like that." When she nodded, he explained, "My mother means well. I think she's always sensed that deep down I didn't feel like I truly belonged. And when she saw that she couldn't give that to me, she looked for others to give it to me, namely women."

The darkness and her averted head hid her facial expression and he found that he desperately needed to see her face when he bared his soul. "Cassie, I know this is difficult. If you can't give me anything else, at least look at me."

She lifted her watery eyes to his, and he ran a thumb over her trembling lips.

"I love you. You've made me happier than I've ever been. And I want you to marry me."

He watched her squeeze her eyes shut, and the tears streamed down her cheeks. "Those don't look like tears of joy."

She gulped down a sob, and he pulled her into his arms, knowing this was the last time he would hold her. He kissed the tears away, and she shook her head, whispering brokenly, "I'm so sorry, but I just can't."

"I . . . love you." Her aqua eyes shone only with pain, and Joshua felt his heart rent in two when he felt her retreat. Gently, she removed her hands from him and moved away.

"I just can't."

Clenching his jaw at the onslaught of emotions, he nodded. "I understand."

He smiled sadly. "I never thought I'd love someone enough to commit myself, but you've changed all that." When pain slashed across her face again, he shook his head. "Don't be sad for me, love. Because, even though I feel ripped to shreds right now, I wouldn't trade one moment I've had with you."

He reached over and kissed her lips; imprinting in his memory this last taste, smell, and feel of her. His tongue claimed the recesses of her sweet lips one last time and then he pulled away, feeling the moisture from his own eyes upon his cheeks. "You've set me free, pretty lady. I only hope you'll find someone who can set you free, too."

He stood, and without another word walked out of her life.

Cassie didn't bother to drag herself out of bed until noon the next day. Why get out of bed to see how the night had ravaged her face? She'd released her tenuous hold on her emotions and cried so much she'd almost made herself sick. It was the first time she'd cried herself to sleep in years, and Cassie found herself thinking of ways to avoid looking in the mirror. Her eyes felt like someone had stretched their sockets entirely too far. Her skin was irritated by the dried moisture of her tears, and her body felt limp.

Easing from her bed, she scowled at the sunlight and placed herself in front of a soothing warm shower, hoping the pulsing water would transform her into a human again. Her thoughts flitted back to the previous evening, and pain sliced through her like a sharp blade. If only he had shouted at her, acted smug, or been coolly remote. But he had made himself vulnerable to her and comforted her, when she knew his own pain must have been unbearable.

If only she could commit and be what he needed. Cassie shook her head in defeat. But she couldn't. Joshua deserved her honesty, and she would have felt like a fraud if she agreed to marry him. Who are you kidding, a little voice said. You wanted your relationship to last forever, too. You were just too much of a coward to admit it or risk it.

"Coward!" she said out loud. Never having been accused of cowardice, she found herself extremely uncomfortable with the label and turned her mind to other things, like food. She might feel like she was dead, but her stomach was protesting otherwise. So, Cassie made a half-hearted attempt at eating a plate of scrambled eggs and toast and sighed over her melancholy. Is this what she had to look forward to?

In the next few days, Cassie discovered, much to her distress and pain, how many ways one person could miss another. Namely, how many ways Cassie could miss Joshua. She missed his impromptu visits to her shop. She missed the way he teased her. She missed the way they'd shared their past secrets with each other.

And the nights were the pits.

Each morning, she'd wake, unconsciously reaching for him only to fill her hands with nothing.

Initially, she made elaborate efforts to avoid seeing him, parking around the block from her shop so that she didn't have to walk past his store. She took her lunch inside the store so she wouldn't accidentally meet him on the sidewalk. Then, she chided herself for her childishness and went back to parking her car in her old space.

When Cassie hadn't seen Joshua for several days, she found her behavior changing from avoidance to seeking. She totally disgusted herself by straining for a glimpse of him. Withdrawal, she thought irritably. When one person got used to being with another person, it would be natural to have a period of withdrawal. She'd give it a week or two and she wouldn't be feeling this incredible urge to park herself in front of Joshua's business so that she could study his face; make sure his eyes were the same warm brown, check the cleft in his chin.

Impatient with her distraction, she called Kim and arranged to meet her for lunch. They met at a loud, busy deli that didn't encourage intimate conversation, but that didn't seem to affect Kim. After they collected their sandwiches and sat down, Kim made a clucking noise and felt Cassie's forehead as if to check for fever. "Honey, you must be sick to turn away a man like Joshua Daniels. Go see your doctor before it's too late."

Cassie sighed. So much for getting rid of her distraction. "It's too late."

"Why?" asked Kim emphatically. "Why? Why? Why?"

"He thinks he wants to get married and I don't."

"Like I said, why? Why? Why?"

Cassie shrugged. "I don't know why he thinks he wants to marry me. I mean—"

Kim rolled her eyes heavenward. "No, silly. Why don't you want to marry him?" She looked at Cassie carefully and narrowed her eyes. "This doesn't have anything to do with his bum father, does it?"

Cassie stared at Kim in astonishment. "No! What does his father have to do with anything?"

"Well," Kim said hesitantly, "some people have problems with stuff like that. I didn't really figure you for that type, but you never know."

"You're kidding." Cassie continued defensively. "I can't imagine why anyone wouldn't want to associate with Joshua. He's kind, strong, and he has an enormous amount of integrity." *Besides having the sexiest brown eyes she'd ever seen,* she added silently.

"So, why don't you want to uh . . . associate with him on a permanent basis?"

"You mean, because he says he thinks he wants to marry me?"

Kim took a sip of her cola and narrowed her eyes again. "You keep saying thinks. Did Joshua say he thinks or is this something you've added?"

"Well, no," Cassie said hesitantly as she stirred her drink with her straw. "He didn't say he thought he wanted to marry me. He said he wanted to marry me."

After swallowing a bite of her pita, Kim observed, "Sounds like you're not too sure. Has he ever said or done anything to suggest that he was unsure? I mean, has he tried to conceal your relationship from his family or his friends or anything like that?''

''Well, no,'' Cassie answered and then paused. ''He's been pretty forthright. It's just that . . .'' Cassie wondered if she should discuss this with Kim, but decided to continue. She'd felt too lonely and burdened for too long.

''Kim, you know that I was once engaged.'' Kim nodded encouragingly and Cassie continued, ''Well, the wedding was called off one day before because Billy Joe had gotten this other girl pregnant.''

Cassie watched Kim's eyes widen in horror as she finished her account of her disastrous experience with near-matrimony.

Kim blew a little whoosh of air through her lips. ''I can see where that might put you off men for awhile.''

Then, after swallowing her last bite, Kim said, ''But you can't go on believing that behind every man lurks the spirit of Billy Joe. Plus, look at how much younger you were. Don't you think your judgment in men has improved a little over time?''

Cassie considered that carefully. ''I don't know,'' she answered slowly. ''I just know that when someone starts talking about weddings I get a queasy feeling in the pit of my stomach, like when you get stuck at the top of the Ferris wheel because it's temporarily broken.''

''So,'' Kim clarified gently, ''what you're really saying is that you're not so much afraid of commitment as you are the marriage ceremony. In other words, you could happily commit to living with Joshua the rest of your life if it didn't involve a marriage ceremony.''

The truth hit Cassie like a glass of cold water in the

face. The light turned on in her brain. Of course, she'd always known she'd been particularly sensitive about weddings since Billy Joe. And Joshua had tried to point out her extreme fear, but she'd been unable to admit it. If Joshua hadn't brought up marriage, she would have followed him to the ends of the earth if that's what he wanted. Isn't that how married people were supposed to feel?

She turned her attention back to Kim with a vague smile. "You're right. I love Joshua and I want to be with him all of the time." Her happiness at the realization that her fear was not with commitment but with marriage faded.

"But, it still doesn't do us any good," she explained glumly. "He wants to get married and I don't."

"You don't want to go through a marriage cere- mony," Kim corrected.

"Yes," Cassie said slowly. "So?"

Her perky friend tossed her dark hair and chided, "There's always Las Vegas. I mean, the only anticipa- tion time would be the plane ride. The wedding could be over in less than five minutes." Kim reached over and patted Cassie's hand. "Look, if I'm late again from lunch, my manager will probably lock me in the bank vault, so I've got to run." Kim smiled. "You think about what I said." Then she giggled mischievously. "Besides, if you elope, it might prompt Fred a little bit. Let me know what happens." Blowing a kiss to the air, she hustled her way through the crowd leaving Cassie with her uneaten sandwich in front of her and plenty of food for thought.

Cassie chewed on her sandwich and Kim's words. The noisy lunch crowd faded and thoughts of Joshua overwhelmed her. Perhaps their relationship wasn't hopeless. Perhaps they could work something out between them. Cassie grimaced at the notion of running off to Las Vegas. She finished her lunch with the realization that she was hopelessly, desperately, eternally in love with Joshua Daniels. She needed to resolve her fear of weddings before she could face him. But resolve it, she decided firmly, she must.

Cassie spent the next weekend immersed in taking care of her store. With the huge success of her grand opening, she'd had to reorder. The merchandise was delivered and because Maggie took the weekend to visit her new grandchild, the work fell to Cassie alone. But in spite of the heavy workload, Joshua stood, like an immovable object, at the forefront of her mind. She found it took twice as long to complete a task when her mind was firmly planted on the man who had brought her life such joy, and by Monday she was exasperated with herself.

Joshua passed her window and Cassie stopped her answer to a customer's question, mid-sentence, staring after his tall form. Maggie nudged her back to reality with a loud cough, and Cassie absently finished the transaction. When Maggie brought up the subject of Joshua later that day, Cassie gently refused to discuss him. She was confused enough without another person's opinion, even sweet Maggie's.

On Tuesday, she came into the shop, still feeling unresolved and restless. The day progressed normally, until Maggie walked in with a worried frown on her face. The older woman was shaking her head.

Chiding herself on her self-absorption, Cassie shifted

her concern to Maggie. "What's wrong, Maggie? Is everything well with your daughter and grandson?"

Maggie looked up at Cassie and chewed her gum thoughtfully. "No, my grandson's just fine." The older woman shook her head. "It's Mr. Daniels, next door. He practically mowed me down on the sidewalk. Said something about an emergency. He's usually real mannerly. Must be—"

Cassie froze at the mention of Joshua's name. Then, she clutched Maggie's shoulders and interrupted the older woman's musings. "What else did he say? What kind of emergency?"

Maggie wore a baffled expression. "Well, I don't know. He was in a big hurry. Wait, I think he said something about his father." Her eyebrows furrowed in confusion. "But, I thought you told me that his daddy died."

"Yes, but . . ." Cassie's voice trailed off. He must have been talking about his biological father, she thought. Then she realized how tightly she was gripping Maggie's shoulders and released them. Dismayed, she apologized, "Oh, I'm sorry, Maggie. I wasn't thinking."

Maggie patted Cassie's shoulder awkwardly. "Aw, that's okay. I know Joshua's special to you, even though you two haven't had the sense to work out your problems."

Cassie smiled and admitted, "Yes, he is special to me." Pausing only a moment, she said, "Listen, I suspect that Joshua could be going through a rough time right now, and I don't want him to be alone. Would you mind covering for me?"

Maggie grabbed Cassie's purse and practically shoved

her out the door. "Of course not. You get on along and take care of your man." Calling after Cassie a moment later, she ordered, "You just make sure you send me an invitation."

Cassie turned back around, waiting for the familiar panic, but she felt only concern for Joshua and a peaceful serenity in knowing that she would be with him shortly. She grinned and nodded, then she dashed into Joshua's store to question his clerk.

Joshua sat in the empty hospital chapel silently shaking his head. Lord! What a morning. He was still trying to comprehend the strange confession Harry had given him while the old man lay in the emergency room bed. Only, the old guy's name wasn't Harry, it was Clement. The more he tried to figure it out, the harder his head pounded in rebellion. Resting his elbows on his knees, he pinched the bridge of his nose and exhaled slowly. He heard the door whisper open and his only thought was that he hoped whoever had joined him in the chapel would respect his privacy.

A wisp of familiar fragrance teased his nostrils and his head involuntarily turned toward the intruder.

His heart slammed against his ribs at the sight of her. He must be dreaming. Joshua rubbed his eyes to make certain that he hadn't gone completely over the edge and was suffering delusions. But there she stood, just as she did in his dreams. And his nightmares, for that matter. Just last night, he'd dreamed of holding her in his arms, only to have her disappear into a fine mist.

She wore a flowing pink skirt and a coordinating blouse with a lace collar. Her honeyed hair was pulled back from her lovely face with pink combs. And the aqua eyes he'd lost himself in so many times before showed a mixture of concern and tentativeness.

"Joshua," she said softly, "I heard about your father. Is he going to be all right?"

"Yes," he answered absently, wondering who could have told her. "How did you know?"

She gave a little smile and sat next to him on the edge of the bench. "Well, Maggie tipped me off and—"

Comprehension dawned and Joshua nodded. "Yeah, I practically knocked her down I was in such a hurry."

Joshua wondered if that was the only reason she was here. His heart beat faster with the hope that she had possibly changed her mind about their relationship. Had she missed him half as much as he'd missed her?

Stealing a surreptitious glance at her, he noticed her hands were situated in her lap, clasping and unclasping her fingers. The tiny hope grew larger at this sign of nervousness, and he swallowed down his own anxiety. The silence between them stretched to uneasiness and because he could resist no longer, he reached his large hand over to cover her delicate fidgeting ones.

At his touch, she looked into his face then down at their hands. Carefully, she pulled her hands away and his breath stopped when he thought she might push him away.

But she didn't. Instead, using both of her hands, she twined her fingers with his and held his hand firmly.

She looked back into his face and her eyes spoke a vow more eloquently than words could express. His chest tightened and ached with emotion, but he needed the words. He asked in a rough voice, "Why are you here?"

She whispered, "Because I love you."

He closed his eyes and whispered a silent prayer. "For how long?"

"Forever."

His heart burst for joy and he pulled her into his arms. "Ah, Cassie."

"I'm so sorry, Joshua." Her voice broke and her eyes filled with unshed tears. "I've been foolish. But I was so terrified of risking my heart again that I didn't realize I'd already given it to you. Can you ever forgive me?"

"Oh, God, yes." He stroked her cheek with wonder. "Just tell me this isn't a dream."

She gave him a watery smile and tightened her arms around his neck. "It's no dream."

He pulled back and stared into her eyes for reassurance. "And it's not temporary. I won't demand marriage from you if you insist, but it's got to be permanent. I couldn't handle you walking out of my life again." She looked away, and Joshua's heart sank. Had he misread her? Hadn't she said forever?

He shook her gently. "Cassie, talk to me."

Her heart was in her eyes when she quietly replied. "What if I want you to demand marriage?"

Shocked, he said, "But—"

Then, with a touch of defiance, she said, "What if I insist?"

He knew his face wore a silly smile, and he was having difficulty remaining coherent. "Uh," he stumbled over his thoughts, "that's fine with me. Can we do it quickly while you're in this frame of mind?" His mind worked rapidly. "We could go to the justice of the peace tomorrow . . . or better yet, we could fly out to Vegas.''

Her laugh took him by surprise, and he studied her inquisitively.

''I had lunch with Kim the other day,'' Cassie explained. ''We talked all of this out and she suggested Vegas. But I don't think we should take off for Las Vegas with your father in the hospital.''

Joshua was quiet for a moment, then he shook his head. ''I don't know if you're ready for this. But that wasn't my father.''

Totally confused, Cassie repeated, ''Not your father?''

''No, his name is Clement Brown and he knew my father before he died.''

''Your father's dead?''

''Yes,'' Joshua nodded. ''Do you remember me telling you about how I didn't recognize my father when he showed up during my teenage years?'' When she nodded, he continued, ''Well, the reason I didn't recognize him is because he wasn't my biological father. He met Harry, my real father, after Harry recovered from alcoholism and started a shelter for alcoholic men.''

Joshua smiled and pulled her closer into his arms. ''Apparently, Harry showed Clement my picture and told him how proud he was of me. He said I looked so much like my mom that it used to tear his heart out to look at me. Anyway, Harry told Clement that alcohol had ruined his chances with me and that he hoped Clement would get into a recovery center so that he wouldn't miss out on all that life had to offer.''

Sadly, Joshua shook his head. ''Clement really looked up to Harry, and when Harry died, he made a vow to tell me what had become of my father. But when he came around me, he found he had this fantasy of having a son like me and couldn't tell me the truth.'' Joshua shrugged. ''This morning, he got hit by a car and was afraid I'd never learn the truth about Harry. He had the hospital call me. When I got to the emergency room, he blurted out this story, complete with a baby picture of me. He was relieved that I wasn't angry with him.''

''Gosh, what a story.''

''I know.'' Joshua grinned. ''The neat thing is that now I know my father didn't remain a bum. He redeemed himself and helped a lot of other people. And Clement has finally agreed to sign himself into a rehabilitation center.''

Cassie turned and studied him. ''So, how do you feel about all this?''

''Stunned . . . and relieved.''

''Relieved?''

''Yeah, I'd always felt this strange burden about my father's alcoholism, as if I were responsible. But Harry told Clement that he'd had problems with the bottle long before my mother died. I didn't ever really know him. But I'm glad he got his life straightened out.''

Cassie's heart overflowed with love for Joshua. She touched his strong jaw and smiled. ''You look glad.''

He moved her hand to his lips and kissed her fingers. ''The true story of Harry and Clement is only responsible for a small measure of my happiness. You're the one who really turned my life around.'' He chuckled, and the vibration sent goose bumps along her arms. ''Of course, you've turned it upside down, too. So, take your pick: Las Vegas today or the justice of the peace tomorrow. Which one will it be?''

He wore an expectant expression, and Cassie shook her head. ''Joshua, I told your mother we weren't going to elope. I think she'd be terribly offended if we didn't include her in our plans.''

His eyebrows drew together in a frown. ''I don't want to wait. I'm afraid you'll change your mind.''

Her heart beat wildly at his possessive gaze, and she didn't care that she wore her heart on her sleeve. ''My mind and heart can't be changed.'' Helplessly, she reassured him, ''I belong to you, now.''

Joshua groaned and claimed her mouth with his hungry lips.

EPILOGUE

Fussing with her hair one last time, Cassie gazed into the mirror with a mixture of awe and joy. Joshua had barely given her time to breathe, let alone get jitters over the wedding. Ten days had passed since that fateful morning they'd shared together in the hospital chapel. Ten days since he'd delegated the planning of the wedding to his mother and Cassie's mother. Both women had been delighted with the opportunity to pull off such an occasion and spent hours on the phone getting acquainted with each other while making the arrangements. The only decision Cassie had been required to make was the selection of her dress.

She'd found it in a little shop down the street from her own store. It was a sample that fit her perfectly, and Kim had cried when she watched Cassie model it. The fitted lace bodice molded flatteringly to her breasts and billowed to her feet in a swirl of crisp, white organdy. She was thankful that the material draped briefly over her shoulders because the temperature outside was quite warm for September.

"Cassie," Kim called her out of her reverie. "Here are two presents from Joshua."

"Two?" Cassie took both wrapped packages and stared at them in confusion.

"Well, don't keep us in suspense, go ahead," Marie urged.

She unwrapped the large square one and laughed when she realized what it was. A dart game. The note said: "Cassie, my love, You stole my heart during a dart game. We can spend the rest of our lives competing with this silly board as long as you know that every time I win, your love will be my prize." It was signed "Your Joshua."

Cassie felt the tears fill her eyes for the bezillionth time that morning, and Kim clucked over her, admonishing her not to muss her makeup.

Shakily, she unwrapped the small jeweler's box and gave up on stopping the flow of tears that streamed down her face. The heart-shaped diamond ring fit her finger to perfection, and she distantly heard the murmured approval of her friends. They hadn't had time to get an engagement ring, and Cassie had decided that they would exchange wedding bands. But he had obviously taken the time to go shopping and get the ring fitted expressly for her. The heart reminded her of Joshua, and she vowed to treasure him, to keep him safe within her love.

"Fix your face, Cassie," Kim said, her own eyes suspiciously bright. "They're playing your song."

*   *   *

Joshua shifted from foot to foot. Shoving his clenched hands into his pockets, he tried to conceal his anticipation. Tom, Fred, and Jack reassured him with indulgent whispers.

When the wedding march began, his heart lodged in his throat. He fought against the fear that she'd get cold feet and leave him at the altar. Then he grinned at his thoughts. What altar? The wedding was outdoors with guitars for accompaniment, folding chairs, and bouquets of flowers brought in by the local florist.

He'd done everything in his power to make this experience different from Cassie's disaster with Billy Joe, although he thanked God everyday that she hadn't married him. He'd barely left her side during the last ten days. And only with the understanding that Kim would stay with her last night, did he reluctantly spend his last night as a bachelor at his mother's home.

He nodded vaguely to Kim, Marie, and Anne as they made their way down the aisle, but his breath stopped when he saw Cassie move from behind a stand of trees to be escorted by her father. She was a vision in white holding red sweetheart roses. Her wispy veil, edged in delicate lace, framed her face to reveal a radiance that rivalled the sun. His gaze locked with hers, and they exchanged their promises silently before they made their vows public.

When she reached him, her father kissed her on the cheek and joined Cassie's hand with his. They faced each other, and the aura of their love spilled out onto the happy guests. With the prompting of the minister, they exchanged their vows and the time came for Joshua to claim his bride with a kiss. The kiss was a pledge: emotional, passionate, and long enough for a few of the guests to twitter and murmur among themselves. When he broke away, he saw that Cassie's eyes were as dazed as he felt.

In a low voice intended for only her ears, he asked, "How long do we have to stay at the reception? The honeymoon suite at the St. James Inn is waiting impatiently, Mrs. Daniels."

Amusement sparkled from her eyes. "I think you're confused, Mr. Daniels. A room cannot be impatient. And I know you can't be impatient since we've only had one night apart."

"Ah, but there's a difference. Now you're my bride."

Her blood heated as it always did when Joshua looked at her with that sensual intensity, and she understood that he wanted to make his possession complete.

All of a sudden, Joshua swept her into his arms and twirled her around. And they shared an intimate laugh because both their fears had finally been put to rest.

Joshua knew without a doubt that he truly belonged, as he always would, to Cassie.

And Cassie saw the bright promise of her future in a pair of warm, brown eyes that shone only for her.